MW00388846

MY MISSION

M AX1M UM G1R L

Dark Angel

The Eyes Only Dossier

Logan Cale

compiled by D. A. Stern

ballantine books • new york

A Del Rey® Book
Published by The Ballantine Publishing Group

www.delreydigital.com

ISBN 0-345-45185-6

Book Design by Laura Lindgren

Manufactured in the United States of America

First Edition: February 2003

10 9 8 7 6 5 4 3 2 1

Dark Angel
The Eyes Only Dossier

May 28, 2021

Matt—

Good to hear from you again. Clemente seems like a stand-up guy, and he may be one of the few honest cops on the force, but I'm glad you're back in town. We can use all the friends we can get.

The person who just handed you this package is named Cain. He understands English, even if he can't speak it, and he's been given explicit instructions to give this to Detective Matt Sung, Seattle Metro Police—no one else. You know what will happen to him if he's caught outside the fence—get him safely back to the fence, if you would. Thanks.

You should be alone when you look at the material you now possess. If it fell into the wrong hands, what's in it could cost some people their lives. I'm taking a big risk just sending it to you like this.

But at this point, I may not have any choice. And you're one of the few people I can trust completely.

As I write this, army troops outside the fence are massing near the two main entrances. Don't know if they're just flexing their muscles again, or if they really intend to use the tanks this time, but everyone here is preparing for a fight to the finish. I don't think the boys in green will just start shooting—but I'm sure they'll be able to find a pretext to begin the attack, if that's what they decide they want to do.

People here are anxious as well—the water got cut off again, and most of our other supplies are running low as well.

This morning at breakfast I got a look from Cat Lady that made me feel like Tweety Bird. Got the same kind of look from a few of the other transgenics as well, like I was far enough down the evolutionary ladder to be part of the food chain.

No—that's not fair. Everybody's gone out of their way to help me fit in—make me feel like one of them, even if I'm not. Makes me feel good—like coming here was the right decision.

I've been using a landline from my new digs to tie in to the Informant Net—but yesterday afternoon, somebody out there must have cut it. Third time this week that happened. I'll get it fixed soon, I'm sure, but for the moment I'm deaf, dumb, and blind to the outside world—and to the Net. Everything I've been working on is stopped dead in its tracks. And that can't happen. Lives are at stake.

I'm trusting you to make certain the work goes on—even if I don't. In the package are files on the four most critical investigations I've been working on, as well as instructions on whom you should consider passing the material on to. I've laid things out so that whoever's looking at the files can see how the investigations played out—and decide which leads to follow up on. Some of these things you already know. Others you don't. You'll see.

Sorry to lay all this on you, my friend—but we both knew this day might come. If you don't hear from me again, you know what to do.

Stay strong. Fight on.

Logan

SECTOR 55

Sector 55

Crossfile:

Margaret Curran

Rollins Miller

Sand Point Redevelopment Corporation

The Pacific Free Press

Tuesday, October 18, 2016 * 50 Cents

CURRAN MISSING!

Mayoral Candidate Disappears En Route to Staff Meeting; Apparent Kidnapping

Mayoral Candidate Margaret Curran

SON ILYA, CAMPAIGN CHAIR HARRISON BOTH KILLED

by Logan Cale

SEATTLE—With just a little more than three weeks remaining until Election Day, Green Party candidate Margaret Curran—locked in a virtual dead heat with four-term incumbent mayor Rene Beltran—was apparently abducted last night on the way to a staff meeting at her Fremont campaign headquarters.

The bodies of Curran's son, Ilya, and Campaign Chairperson April Harrison were found in Ms. Curran's bullet-riddled limousine at approximately 11:12 P.M., according to police department spokesperson Carly Tulloch.

"We're still going over the crime scene," Tulloch said in a statement issued this morning, "but at this time we're treating this as a kidnapping. We have every reason to believe Ms. Curran is still alive, and are committed to finding her and bringing the people responsible for these crimes to justice."

Details of the crime remain sketchy. While awaiting more information, the mayor himself issued a brief statement, extending his sympathies to the Curran and Harrison families and promising to throw the full weight of his office behind the search for the criminals.

The kidnapping is the latest in a series of events that have made this year's mayoral race the most eventful campaign in recent memory. Two weeks ago, the Republican candidate, businessman Arturo Gutierrez, voluntarily withdrew from the race, stating that his presence on the ballot would virtually guarantee a win for Curran. The next day, Curran produced evidence that Gutierrez and Beltran had met several times preceding that announcement, and accused them of "sandbagging the democratic process." Beltran responded by canceling his scheduled debate with Curran; the two continued to exchange acrimonious remarks in the press.

Curran's is the latest and most prominent disappearance in the city over the past year; close to two hundred people, the vast majority of them critics of the Beltran administration, have vanished since January. Whispered rumors of police death squads, given carte blanche to eliminate Mayor Beltran's enemies, have begun to circulate. Not surprisingly, the mayor's allies are already issuing furious denials of any involvement by their candidate.

Ilya Barlow

April Harrison

"This is a tragedy for two families, and for the entire city of Seattle," said City Councilor Leopold Steckler. "I urge all responsible citizens not to compound that tragedy by making ridiculous, unsubstantiated charges of this kind."

However, if Curran remains missing for any length of time, it will in effect guarantee victory for Beltran. And many believe that Curran, a political neophyte, has been on the verge of succeeding where so many before her have failed; that she might be the one to derail the well-oiled Beltran political machine.

Curran began her political career relatively late in life, following the untimely death of her husband, magazine journalist Zane Barlow. Having stayed home to rear the couple's two children, Ilya and younger daughter Asha, Curran first ran for city council in

(see Mayoral Candidate Disappears, p. 8)

To whoever's reading this.

It might be hard to believe—but once upon a time, there was an honest politician in Seattle. Her name was Margaret Curran. When you think about who our elected officials are now—Steckler, and Lans, and Councilor Chambers—you have to wonder what Seattle would be like if Curran hadn't been kidnapped that night, five years ago. If she'd been able to run against Beltran back in 2016. If she'd actually won.

But that wasn't the way it went.

After that night, Curran was never seen again. Beltran got his fourth term, and the police investigation ground to a halt early the following year.

Big surprise.

Her daughter and I never stopped looking, though. After the first few weeks went by, we resigned ourselves to the grim probability that the only thing we would find would be a corpse. After the first few years, we became certain of it.

And then, six weeks ago, I discovered something that showed we might be wrong.

THE
LIGHT IS
PURPLE

ASHA I
LOVE YOU
PLEASE HELP
MARGARET

The note came via the Informant Net—a woman who works in one of the big Harbor Island corrections facilities. She overheard a guard talking at lunch—dumped a tray full of food on him, then used the distraction to steal the note (and his wallet, which came with it).

At first I thought it was a joke. No joke, though—Asha recognized her mother's handwriting.

We did an analysis on it. It was a piece of toilet tissue, industrial-grade, single-ply, that had been folded up into a square the size of a postage stamp. Standard prison issue. The ink had been dry for less than three days.

The woman told us the guard's name: Ray Saunders. We started with him.

TO: iionly@pfpfree.net

FROM: goodsinger@pfpfree.net

DATE: 3/25/21

RE: RAY SAUNDERS

Sorry—I couldn't get anything on this guy besides his service record.

But I can tell you from personal experience that he's a real hardass—the kind of cop that gives the force a bad name. Caught his act one night a few years back, when I was on sector patrol. Beat some kid to within an inch of his life for giving him lip. Then he had the balls to cite the kid for resisting arrest. Busted a light on the back of the kid's car then impounded it. And ***then*** he gave the kid a boot in the ass and sent him on his way.

Nasty.

According to his service record he was part of the riot squad from Sector 7, back in the years right after the Pulse. I'm sure you haven't forgotten how many people went missing after going up against that squad. Those eighteen that vanished in March 2010 are the ones everybody remembers, but they're just the tip of the iceberg.

So yeah—he's a bad apple.

I'll do a little more checking. There seems to be some kind of misprint on the file here. Says he's on special assignment in Sector 55.

But there's no Sector 55 in Seattle.

I'll be in touch.

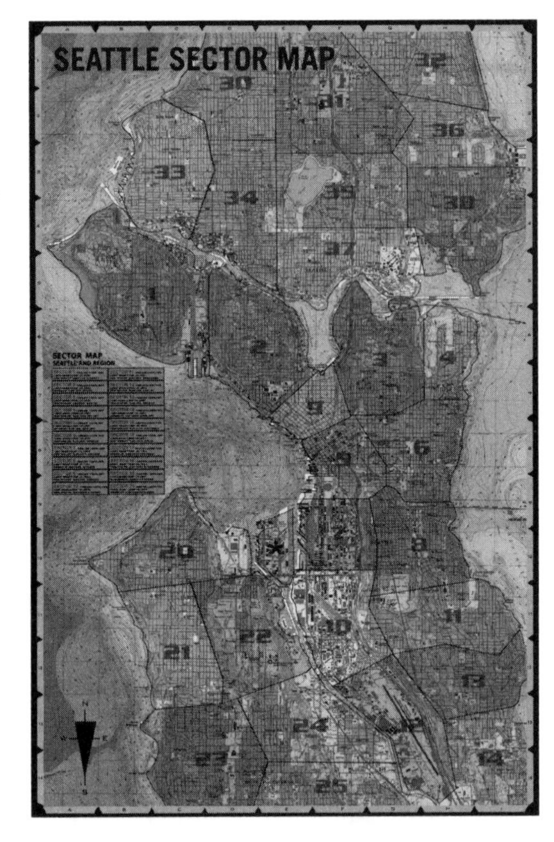

Form 2156-G (Replaces 2155) *

SEATTLE POLICE SERVICE RECORD

Name:	Raymond Saunders
Employee I.D.:	Badge 489G-3
CAD#:	358993
Employment date:	11/5/08
Rank:	Sergeant
Division/Bureau/Unit:	Special Assignment Sector 55
Height:	6'2"
Weight:	220
Certificates/licenses:	Distinguished Service Cross 5/15 Distinguished Service Cross 7/15 Marksman 3—4/12 Marksman 2—8/13 Marksman 1—1/14
Promotion history:	Patrolman 1st Class—8/12 Sergeant—9/14
Current assignments:	Restricted Information
Previous assignments:	Sector 7 Riot Squad Sector 7 Checkpoint Reinforcement Sector 18 Station Security Harbor Island Penitentiary Guard Harbor Island Penitentiary Block Supervisor
Medical history:	Cert. 4G—Col A+
Date of last physics:	1/8/21
Blood type:	A+
Address:	34—17 N.E. 78th Street Seattle WA
Phone:	206-48744
E-mail:	rsaunders@seattle.pd.gov
Emergency contact:	Johanna Saunders (sister)
Next appraisal/review date:	11/5/2021
Termination information:	N.A.

DECRYPTION: SECURE 8 DECRYPTION STAMP: 5/8/21 ORIGINAL TRANSCRIPT: 4/1/21 L = Cale, Logan, A = Barlow, Asha

INTERROGATION TRANSCRIPT

FILE BEGINS

L: He's coming around. Make sure the scarf is tight.

Saunders: What is this, some kind of April Fool's crap? Is that you, Addy?

L: I'm not Addy.

Saunders: Yeah. I hear that. Where am I?

L: Someplace no one's ever going to find you.

Saunders: Really?

L: Really. It took us a long time to track you down, Ray. You're not getting out of here until you answer our questions.

Saunders: Uh-huh. Then I guess you'd better start asking.

L: Where's Margaret Curran?

Saunders: Who?

L: Margaret Curran. You had a note from her in your wallet.

Saunders: So you're the shit who stole my wallet.

L: I wouldn't worry about that right now, if I were you. I'd just concentrate on answering my questions.

Saunders: You're the one who oughtta start worrying, you little prick. I don't know who you are, but you're making a serious mistake here. Let me go now, or—

A: You're making a serious mistake if you don't start talking.

Saunders: Ah, a chick. I thought there was more than one of you in here. Who the hell are you?

L: We're asking the questions, Ray. Now, where's Margaret Curran?

Saunders: Like I said, I don't know who the hell she is, and I don't know anything about a goddamn—

A: A little piece of tissue paper. Folded up in your wallet.

Saunders: That? One of the other guards gave it to me.

L: Which one?

Saunders: I don't remember.

L: When did he give it to you?

Saunders: I don't remember that, either.

L: Come on, Ray. You're a smart guy—I've seen your record. Think a little bit harder.

Saunders: That's the best I can do. Sorry, chief.

A: Maybe we can help jog your memory.

Saunders: What, you got a baseball bat back there, or something? That's not gonna help.

L: Not a bat, Ray.

Saunders: Hey!

L: Just a little something to help loosen your tongue.

Saunders: Oh, Christ. Oh hell. What did you do?

L: Relax, Ray. It's just a little dopamine. Now why don't you tell us everything you know about Margaret Curran.

Saunders: Oh goddamn it. Goddamn you.

A: Cut the crap, Ray. Tell us what you know about Margaret Curran. About Sector 55.

Saunders: (Unintelligible)

L: Hey, hold on. Something's wrong.

A: He's faking.

L: I don't think so. Ray! What is it?

Saunders: (Unintelligible)

A: I'll get Leonard.

FILE CONTINUES

DECRYPTION: SECURE 8 DECRYPTION STAMP: 5/8/21 ORIGINAL TRANSCRIPT: 4/1/21 L = Cale, Logan, A = Barlow, Asha

TO: Jsaunders48@seattle.gov

FROM: iionly@pfpfree.net

DATE: 4/3/21

RE: YOUR BROTHER

Please accept my sympathies on your brother Ray's death, Ms. Saunders. I know it must have come as quite a shock. However, there's something you should know about the circumstances of his death. The authorities lied to you. Ray didn't have a heart attack.

They poisoned him—put something in his system that made it impossible for him to tell anyone about what they were having him do—what his real work was. I regret to say I had a hand in what happened to him—an accidental one, but a hand nonetheless.

Check Ray's medical records—if they'll let you. You'll find that I'm telling the truth.

I will contact you again.

—A friend.

TO: iionly@pfpfree.net

FROM: Jsaunders48@seattle.gov

DATE: 4/3/21

RE: YOUR BROTHER

"Friend"—

Whatever kind of trouble you're peddling I don't need. Leave me alone.

TO: Jsaunders48@seattle.gov

FROM: iionly@pfpfree.net

DATE: 4/3/21

RE: YOUR BROTHER

My mistake—I thought you cared about Ray.

TO: iionly@pfpfree.net

FROM: Jsaunders48@seattle.gov

DATE: 4/3/21

RE: YOUR BROTHER

Where the hell do you get off "Friend" you don't know the first thing about me.

TO: Jsaunders48@seattle.gov

FROM: iionly@pfpfree.net

DATE: 4/4/21

RE: YOUR BROTHER

You're wrong, Ms. Saunders. I know everything about you.

Your Social Security # is 909-924-9932-21.

You live at 476 Collingwood, Number 12B.

You work downtown, for Colson Import/Export, in sales. Next week you're up for a promotion to district manager. You're not going to get it—your boss already sent a memo to the company president.

Your parents died in the first year of rioting, after the Pulse. Ray took care of you, used his connections to get you your apartment, to get rid of that guy who was harassing you at your old job, to make your life as easy, as good as he could. He looked out for you, Ms. Saunders. Look out for him now.

Help me find out why he died—what he was doing that was so important he had to walk around with poison in his veins.

TO: iionly@pfpfree.net

FROM: Jsaunders48@seattle.gov

DATE: 4/4/21

RE: YOUR BROTHER

Oh God I know who you are now I should have guessed by that e-mail address. Ha ha mr last free voice.

You can afford to say anything you want. nobody knows who you are. I can't say a thing.

TO: Jsaunders48@seattle.gov

FROM: iionly@pfpfree.net

DATE: 4/4/21

RE: YOUR BROTHER

Yes, you can.

All replies to this address go through a server that replaces I.P. headers and machine I.D.'s with random characters—renders you anonymous.

Tell me what Ray was doing.

TO: iionly@pfpfree.net

FROM: Jsaunders48@seattle.gov

DATE: 4/4/21

RE: YOUR BROTHER

I can't believe I'm writing this.

I don't know anything about what Ray was doing these last few years. But I know who he was doing it for. Rollins Miller, Chief Miller.

I'm sure you remember him.

LATE EDITION

Seattle Post

THE VOICE OF PUGET SOUND

****

Monday, November 2, 2015

23 Cents Plus Tax

NOT GUILTY!!!

Miller, Lans, Kaffaffian All Walk
Speers Throws Out Case Against Police "Death Squads"

by Hunter Dylan

In a ruling that sparked violent protests throughout the city of Seattle, Judge George H. Speers yesterday morning dismissed all charges against three officials accused of running the police force's infamous "death squads." These units—whose existence has never been proven—were rumored to be responsible for the disappearance of dozens of persons who vanished without a trace as far back as 2010.

Citing the 2010 laws that established the Military Protectorate of Seattle, as well as martial law ordinances specific to the James-Cheney Act, Speers ruled that the internal department memoranda used to indict Chief Rollins Miller, Deputy Commissioner Alan Lans, and Deputy Chief Greg Kaffaffian had been illegally obtained. Without the paper trail tying the two men to activities committed by sector forces, Speers declared, the prosecution's case was nonexistent.

District Attorney Eva Richardson was quick to respond to the ruling. In a statement released by her office, Richardson called the decision "a travesty of justice" and promised a swift appeal. Relatives of those who had disappeared packed the courtroom every day of the months-long trial, and many were more vocally angry about the judge's decision.

"I don't know what the hell country I'm living in anymore," snapped James Carter, a retired contractor whose two sons—Sean and James Jr.—were among those who vanished late last year during the so-called Coffeehouse Crackdowns in Sector 5. "The law's supposed to help out people—not kill 'em. Not screw 'em over."

Late yesterday afternoon, angry protesters outside the courthouse burned Speers and the three defendants in effigy. Rioting elsewhere in the neighborhood led Mayor Beltran to briefly cordon off the entire sector and establish a curfew in surrounding areas.

Lans and Kaffaffian were whisked away to waiting cars after the judge's decision, but Chief Miller took a moment to speak with members of the press before leaving the courthouse.

"I have mixed emotions about what happened today, to tell you the truth," Miller said. "I think Judge Speers was correct in his ruling, and yet I would have welcomed—would still welcome—the chance to have my day in court, to prove how groundless these accusations are."

Miller would not, however, address specific questions raised by this paper and the *Portland Intelligencer* concerning the contents of the internal memoranda Speers ruled inadmissable.

The press has obtained copies of these memos; they are currently being vetted by in-house legal counsel. A preliminary review of the memoranda seems to bear out the charges brought by District Attorney Richardson and her staff—that a special police division, under the supervision of Chief Miller and Deputy Commissioner Lans, was responsible for the disappearance of as many as two hundred individuals during the last

Turn to page 12, NOT GUILTY

Miller, Rollins

DOB: 10.24.1968

POB: New Haven CT

MARITAL STATUS: Widowed (wife Rachel
deceased 9.1.2009)

KNOWN RELATIVES: Rollins Jr. (Son),
Andrea (daughter), Karin (daughter)

CURRENT STATUS: Deputy commissioner, Seattle Metro Police
NOTES: Beltran administration holdover.

Chief-death squad connection. (See Pacific Press files/Herman Colberg.)

Possible involvement Dylan, Richardson assassinations.

Residence Capitol Hill Gated Community.

No intel—private security firm, no hack videocams.

Daughter Karin—Seattle Art Trust. Met twice at conservancy benefits. Priss.

THE SEATTLE ART & CONSERVANCY TRUST

April 8, 2021

VIA MESSENGER

Logan Cale
4983 Germaine Towers Penthouse West
Seattle WA

Dear Mr. Cale:

Of course I remember you, and I am very happy to provide you with a schedule (enclosed) of the Trust's 2021 benefit events. May I infer from your inquiry that the recent problems with Cale Industries don't extend to your individual financial situation? I was terribly sorry to hear about your Uncle Jonas, and have been following events in the paper regarding Cale Industries with some concern.

On the possibility of establishing a scholarship in conjunction with the department, I have taken the liberty of mentioning your interest to my father. He suggested that you contact him directly, using his private line, which is 555-222-8759.

Thank you again for your interest in the Trust, and I look forward to seeing you at future events.

Yours sincerely,

Karin Miller
Chairwoman, Events Council

TO: iionly@pfpfree.net

FROM: mac123@pfpfree.net

DATE: 4/9/21

RE: YOUR WISH IS . . .

. . . my command. Next time give me something hard to do.

I'm giving you Miller's phone records from '13 right up through '20, when Steckler reassigned him. Don't know how much these are going to help you, though. Ninety-five percent of the calls on here are internal—to other numbers in the department. EXT. N.A.—extensions not available. Sorry. A flurry of outside calls at the end of '14, beginning of '15—you might want to start there. Most of them to a company called Sand Point Redevelopment Corporation.

This is just about as far back as I can go—the first few years after the Pulse, Northwest has only hard copies. They exist, but you'll have to find someone else to get them for you.

Later.

—Mac

NORTHWEST FIBER OPTIC

Bringing the World Together at the Speed of Light™

PART OF THE PIERPONT LEMKIN FAMILY OF COMPANIES

For Internal Usage Only *** NOT TO BE CIRCULATED

Account # 99902228759
Internal Ref: 2228759
Account Name: Classified
Itemized Call Listing 11-01-14 Through 12-01-14

Sand Point Redevelopment Corporation

No	Date	Time	Location	Number	MIN	TOD	Amount
37	11-01	8:20 A.M.	INTERNAL	EXT. N.A.	1.5	A	.92
38	11-01	8:56 A.M.	SEATTLE WA	*206-5181-2639	14.0	A	8.54
39	11-01	12:21 P.M.	INTERNAL	EXT. N.A.	4.0	A	2.44
40	11-01	5:45 P.M.	SEATTLE WA	*206-5181-2639	23.0	A	14.03
41	11-01	6:15 P.M.	INTERNAL	EXT. N.A	1.5	B	47.50
42	11-02	7:51 A.M.	INTERNAL	EXT. N.A.	3.0	B	.93
43	11-02	4:45 P.M.	SEATTLE WA	*206-5181-2639	12.5	A	7.63
44	11-02	5:10 P.M.	INTERNAL	EXT. N.A.	4.5	A	2.75
45	11-02	6:50 P.M.	SEATTLE WA	206-5181-2639	31.5	B	9.77
46	11-05	8:10 A.M.	INTERNAL	EXT. N.A.	4.0	A	2.44
47	11-05	8:20 A.M.	TACOMA WA	879-2638-4638	4.0	A	2.44
48	11-05	8:44 A.M.	SEATTLE WA	*206-5181-2639	12.0	A	7.32
49	11-05	9:10 A.M.	SEATTLE WA	*206-5181-2639	1.5	A	.92
50	11-05	12:10 P.M.	INTERNAL	EXT. N.A.	8.0	A	4.88
51	11-05	4:36 P.M.	INTERNAL	EXT. N.A.	1.0	A	.61
52	11-05	5:15 P.M.	INTERNAL	EXT. N.A.	1.0	A	.61
53	11-05	5:18 P.M.	SEATTLE WA	*206-5181-2639	14.5	A	8.85
54	11-06	8:10 A.M.	INTERNAL	EXT. N.A	1.5	A	.92
55	11-06	12:10 P.M.	INTERNAL	EXT. N.A.	7.5	A	4.58
56	11-06	12:45 P.M.	INTERNAL	EXT. N.A.	1.0	A	.61
57	11-06	6:10 P.M.	INTERNAL	EXT. N.A.	41.5	B	12.87
58	11-06	7:20 P.M.	SEATTLE WA	*206-5181-2639	13.5	B	4.19
59	11-06	7:34 P.M.	INTERNAL	EXT. N.A.	44.0	B	13.64
60	11-06	8:20 P.M.	SEATTLE WA	*206-5181-2639	14.5	B	4.50
61	11-07	12:10 P.M.	INTERNAL	EXT. N.A.	1.0	A	.61
62	11-07	5:10 P.M.	INTERNAL	EXT. N.A.	1.0	A	.61
63	11-07	5:31 P.M.	INTERNAL	EXT. N.A.	16.5	A	10.07
64	11-07	6:12 P.M.	SEATTLE WA	*206-5181-2639	5.0	B	1.55
65	11-07	6:18 P.M.	INTERNAL	EXT. N.A.	4.5	B	1.40

I've left something out here, I realize. Something that could be critically important.

Whoever you are, if you're from anywhere around Seattle—and you've got a computer—you know about the EYES ONLY Informant Net. On one level, at least. It's a chat room—a safe chat room—a place for people to talk, anonymously, about what's going on in the world. What politicians like Steckler and Beltran, businessmen like Sonrisa and Lemkin, companies like Synthedyne and Arkady Research are doing to our planet. To our city, and our children. You can say whatever you want, and no one can trace you. Secure servers, with constantly shifting I.P. addresses.

But there's a second layer to the Informant Net, a layer that only a few people know about.

That layer consists of a few dozen critically important individuals, people whom I've worked with over the years, who are responsible for getting EYES ONLY the information needed to see that justice is done. People like Mac, who sent me Miller's phone records. Lynn, in the city's corrections department. Gatekeeper, in Homeland Security. Those aren't their real names—just the aliases they go by. I know most of them personally, but their identities have never made it onto any piece of paper. And they never will.

You won't need it to contact them. All you'll need is the following list. I'm passing that on to you as well—with a word of warning.

The system is secure. But not perfect. Be careful with this information.

SOURCE: F:/TEMPFILES/NET/DOSSIERS/LEVEL2/PARTIAL.DBF

LEVEL 2 OPERATIVES

Recruitment Date	E-mail (domain=pfp.free)	Station	Status
XXXXXXXXXXX	troy22	Congressional offices Access schedules, hard copy internal memoranda Limited access Congressional Data Network	Inactive
XXXXXXXXXXX	dazzler	Congressional offices Limited access Congressional Data Network U.S. Senate Archives	Active
XXXXXXXXXXXXXXX	raven	Coroner's Office, City of Seattle All queries	Active
XXXXXXXXXXX	thecolonel	Military Command, State of Washington Limited access, internal network	Indefinitely unavailable
XXXXXXXXXXX	seb2009	Private Tech intel Access foreign and domestic databases Corporate information through SEC records	Active
XXXXXXXXXXXXXXXXX	MsHoney	Seattle P.D., Corrections Limited access Records Office Limited access Security, Harbor Island Complex	Active
XXXXXXXXXXXal	blaze	Seattle Fire Dept. Access internal network Incident videofeed available	Inactive
XXXXXXXXXXX	goodsinger	Seattle P.D. All queries	Active

XXXXXXXXXXXX	deweyd	Library of Congress All archives	Active
XXXXXXXXXXXXXXX	mac123	Northwest Fiber Optic Complete records access Pacific Bell Internet Complete records access	Active
XXXXXXXXXXXX	citizenK	Circuit court offices Limited access, internal network Complete records access, including sealed testimony	Temporary transfer Unavailable until 7/1/21
XXXXXXXXXXXX	ctac	Sea-Tac Airport Control tower logs Customs records	Active
XXXXXXXXXXXX	alias	Port of Seattle Security Tower A Limited import/export manifesto access	Active
XXXXXXXXXXXX	asherman	Seattle Post Archives access Limited access, internal network	Active
XXXXXXXXXXXXXXX	frequentflyer	McChord Air Force Base	Last contact 9/14/20 Presumed Transfer
XXXXXXXXXXXX	gatekeeper	Homeland Security Department Passport Control	Active

FIELDS 5–7 (EMERGENCY CONTACT, EMERGENCY CODE PHRASE, VISUAL DESCRIPTORS) NOT UTILIZED

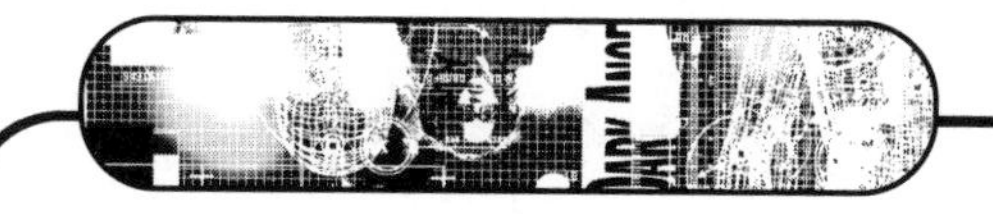

TO: iionly@pfpfree.net

FROM: seb2009@pfpfree.net

DATE: 4/11/21

RE: SAND POINT REDEVELOPMENT CORPORATION

Clever boys, here.

They're playing a shell game with this corporation—it's buried beneath layer after layer of holding companies. And no wonder. Listen to the board of directors: Marbury, Lemkin, Herschler, Liberti. The president is Joann Cappellini. And the chief operations manager is . . .

(drumroll, please)

Rollins Miller.

I have no idea what they're up to, but whatever it is, with rats like that attached, you can bet it stinks.

I'll keep looking.

TO: iionly@pfpfree.net

FROM: thecolonel@pfpfree.net

DATE: 4/10/21

RE: SAND POINT REDEVELOPMENT CORPORATION

Your guess is right—the company name refers to the old military base. See attached—they were given title to most of the prime land up there. I don't think they've done a damn thing with it, though I haven't been up there for a while.

MILITARY PROTECTORATE OF SEATTLE NAVAL BASE REALIGNMENT

Naval Station Puget Sound (Sand Point) at Seattle, WA
MP34:10-Realignment/14-Major

Closure Background
Last Operational Date: 10 Mar 2012

Closure:
Property Summary
Total Acres: 152.00
Acres Disposed: 152.00
Acres Retained: 0.00

DISPOSAL SUMMARY

Parcel Information

Parcel:	Transfer Date:	Method:	Recipient:	Acres:
Parcel 5—Homeless Assistance Area	21 Apr 2012	PBC	City of Seattle	15.00
Parcel 9—Public Roads	11 Aug 2012	NS	City of Seattle	13.50
Parcel 7—UW Student Family Housing	04 Feb 2012	PBC	Sonrisa Foundation	2.00
Parcel 3—Educational Area	04 Feb 2012	PBC	University of Washington	7.50
Parcel 4—Building 9 Educational Area	04 Feb 2012	PBC	University of Washington	5.00
Parcel 8—Biological Resources Division	10 Feb 2012	Fed	Crockett	5.00
Parcel 6—Magnuson Park Expansion Area	18 Mar 2012	NS	Sand Point Redevelopment Corporation	70.00
Parcel 1—North Shore Recreational Area	18 Mar 2012	PBC	City of Seattle	23.00
Parcel 2—North Shore Recreational Area (Building 27)	06 Apr 2013	PBC	City of Seattle	11.00

Disposal Legend

Fed: Fed to Fed
NS: Negotiated Sale
PBC: Public Benefit Conveyance

Activity Timeline

Operational Closure:	First Transfer:	Final Transfer:
10 Mar 2012	21 Apr 2012	06 Apr 2013

Abbreviation Legend

FOST: Finding of Suitability to Transfer
EBS: Environmental Baseline Survey
LRA: Local Redevelopment Authority
EFD/EFA: Engineering Field Division/Engineering Field Activity
RPM/PPM: Real Property Maintenance/Personal Property Maintenance

Extract based on operational data posted through: 01 Jan 2021

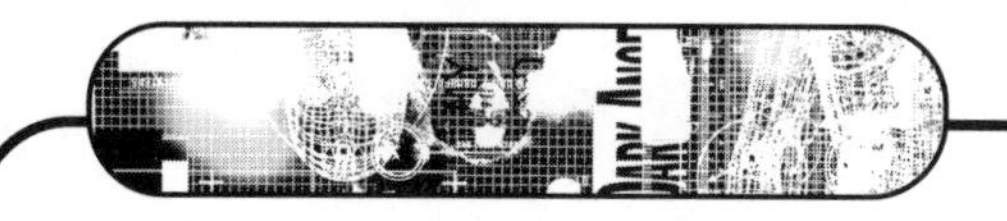

TO: iionly@pfpfree.net

FROM: asherman@pfpfree.net

DATE: 4/12/21

RE: SAND POINT REDEVELOPMENT CORPORATION

All I could find in the archives.

LATE EDITION

Seattle Post

THE VOICE OF PUGET SOUND

23 Cents Plus tax

Friday, April 5, 2013

****

FORMER MILITARY BASE HAS NEW OWNERS

by Stephen Rice
Post Correspondent

Seattle, April 4—Colonel Richard P. Josephson, a spokesman for the Seattle National Guard, announced today a formal transfer of custody with regard to the former military base at Sand Point. Located just outside Seattle, the base, last utilized in the riots of 2009 and 2010 as a holding facility for detainees, has lain vacant since that time.

The Beltran administration, in conjunction with Guard officials, has considered various uses for the site over the last year. One plan proposed the establishment of a "legalized gambling" zone, to include several casinos and a children's theme park. Another—the favorite of many citizens who live in the Sand Point area—called for the creation of an "urban wilderness" retreat. Outright sale of the base to private industry was considered as well.

In the end, the plan announced by Josephson appears to incorporate elements of all those positions, a stance that was echoed by Dona Chernoff, the mayor's spokesman.

"This is a compromise solution—all interested parties, we feel, gained a little something with the plan Colonel Josephson put forth."

Citizens groups blasted the decision as "politics as usual," noting that by far the largest tract of land—the former Magnuson Park area—was transferred outright to a private holding company, the Sand Point Redevelopment Corporation. Chernoff defended that portion of the transfer, saying the corporation will spend millions of dollars on improving the site, something from which "all concerned parties" will benefit.

TO: iionly@pfpfree.net

FROM: seb2009@pfpfree.net

DATE: 4/12/21

RE: SAND POINT REDEVELOPMENT CORPORATION

Re: your query.

No way to get to their bank records. But I know for a fact that they haven't done a damn thing with the land in six years. All that's there—as far as I know—are the old Magnuson Park buildings, and one or two of the detainee barracks from the riots.

I have no idea why they never started development. Maybe they found a use for what was there—as a storage facility, perhaps? Might be worth checking it out.

TO: iionly@pfpfree.net

FROM: goodsinger@pfpfree.net

DATE: 4/10/21

RE: SAND POINT REDEVELOPMENT CORPORATION

What, you don't think I have anything else to do with my time?

I can get out there tomorrow night, take a look around. See what sort of skeletons Miller, Marbury, et al., might have buried in that particular closet.

Too Old to Rock 'n' Roll; Too Young to Die

Is Davis B. Davis giving up music for the mayor's race? **POLITICS**

The Italian Stallion

This heavyweight wants a piece of the action—now

SPORTS

LATE EDITION

Sunday, April 11, 2021

3 Dollars 10 Cents Plus tax

****

Mass Grave Found

18 Bodies Buried at Abandoned Navy Base

by Brooks Johnson
A Post *Exclusive*

April 11—Metro police and a team of forensic scientists from the Seattle coroner's office excavated a grave containing the remains of at least eighteen people on the site of the former Sand Point Naval Station.

Summoned to the deserted base early yesterday evening by an anonymous phone call, authorities arrived to find the grave partially excavated, and the skeletal remains of several persons laid out next to the site.

Sand Point, which served as a holding facility for hundreds of protesters arrested in the widespread rioting that immediately followed the Pulse, was closed down approximately ten years ago. Preliminary testing done by the scientists indicates the grave dates back at least that far, although more precise dating is expected to be done over the next few days. Representatives of the coroner's office also confirmed that DNA would be extracted from the remains and used to identify the bodies.

Representatives of the press were present at the site during the initial phases of excavation, having been informed of the grave's existence by a series of anonymous phone calls, likely from the same caller who brought the site to the authorities' attention. Shortly thereafter, however, the site was sealed off by sector police.

Documents provided anonymously to this newspaper identify the Sand Point Redevelopment Corporation, a company run by a consortium of prominent Seattle businessmen, as the owners of the land where the grave was discovered, though no evidence exists connecting the corporation to the bodies. Former Seattle Police Chief Rollins Miller serves as the chief operations manager of the corporation.

It is not immediately known whether

See Sand Point Grave, p. 21

TO: raven@pfpfree.net

FROM: iionly@pfpfree.net

DATE: 4/12/21

RE: <no subject was specified>

Thanks for getting up there so quickly.

I want to know who those people were.

TO: iionly@pfpfree.net

FROM: raven@pfpfree.net

DATE: 4/12/21

RE: <no subject was specified>

quick note all gunshot deaths no i.d.'s yet .44 caliber police rounds

---

TO: citizenk@pfpfree.net

FROM: iionly@pfpfree.net

DATE: 4/12/21

RE: Sand Point

Keep an eye on this.

TO: iionly@pfpfree.net

FROM: citizenk@pfpfree.net

DATE: 4/13/21

RE: Sand Point

You kidding? I couldn't miss it if I tried. It's all people are talking about over here. The DA's errand boys showed up first thing this morning, picking up warrants. And guess who was number one on their list?

(besides you, that is) ;)

Rollins Miller—the old police chief. Rumors have been floating around for years about his involvement in the March 2010 disappearances—the eighteen people who went up against the riot squads and were never seen again. Eighteen bodies here—that can't be a coincidence, can it?

Whatever's going to happen is going to happen fast. They've already reserved the chief a slot in court—tomorrow a.m.

Somebody wants this over and done with quickly.

Friend of mine is the court reporter—I'll get you the transcript asap.

—K

SEATTLE CIRCUIT COURT
MILITARY PROTECTORATE OF SEATTLE

— — —

Honorable George Herman Speers, Judge Presiding

— — —

MILITARY PROTECTORATE OF SEATTLE, :
PLAINTIFF :
:
VS. :
:
:
ROLLINS A. MILLER, :
DEFENDANT. : NO. CR. 98-012
:

REPORTER'S TRANSCRIPT OF PROCEEDINGS
SEATTLE WASHINGTON
TUESDAY, APRIL 13 2021

APPEARANCES:

FOR THE MILITARY PROTECTORATE OF SEATTLE

Janna Galnick
District Attorney
Steven Ewing Blood
Assistant District Attorney

FOR THE DEFENDANT

Carl Zaccaro Jr.
13–12 4th Street
Seattle WA 98138-0043

Seattle, Washington, On Tuesday, April 16, 2021
Beginning at approximately 9:15 A.M.

THE CLERK: Case 98-012, Military Protectorate of Seattle versus Rollins A. Miller. Counsel, please make your appearance.

MS. GALNICK: ~~Good morning. Janna Galnick and Steven Blood on~~ behalf of the Military Protectorate of Seattle.

MR. ZACCARO: Good morning, Your Honor. Carl Zaccaro representing Rollins A. Miller.

THE COURT: Good morning, Counselors.

THE CLERK: Rollins A. Miller, in case number 98-012, it is alleged that while employed by the Military Protectorate of Seattle as police chief you were involved as an accessory in the murder of eighteen persons. Do you admit or deny said allegations?

THE DEFENDANT: I admit.

MR. ZACCARO: Your Honor, if I may.

THE COURT: Mr. Zaccaro?

MR. ZACCARO: My client wishes to enter a plea of guilty to the charges, and to waive his right to a trial.

THE COURT: Waive his rights?

MR. ZACCARO: He wishes to throw himself on the mercy of the court. He plans to provide information to assist the protectorate in other prosecutions related to this case.

THE COURT: Madame District Attorney, is this acceptable to you?

MS. GALNICK: The defendant's attorney and I have conferenced on this issue, Your Honor, and the protectorate plans to take into consideration any information that is offered by Mr. Miller.

THE COURT: I'd like to know a little bit about what's being offered here. Chief Miller?

THE DEFENDANT: I am prepared to name names—those individuals who committed the actual murders back in '09.

MS. GALNICK: Judge, the protectorate wants to make sure this information is given under oath.

THE COURT: Are you prepared to testify at this point in time, Chief?

THE DEFENDANT: Yes, sir—I am.

THE COURT: Swear the witness.

(Defendant Rollins Miller duly sworn)

THE COURT: All right. Ms. Galnick?

MS. GALNICK: Mr. Blood will begin cross-examination for the protectorate, Your Honor.

THE COURT: Very well. You may proceed.

MR. BLOOD: Thank you, Your Honor. Would you state your full name for the court?

THE DEFENDANT: Rollins Albert Miller.

MR. BLOOD: And from the years 2008 through 2020, you were employed—first by the City of Seattle, and then the protectorate—as Seattle chief of police?

THE DEFENDANT: Yes, sir. That's correct.

MR. BLOOD: Very well. Mr. Miller, I'd like to talk in general first, about July and August 2009—the period immediately following the Pulse.

THE DEFENDANT: It was a terrible time.

MR. BLOOD: Yes, sir. Could you elaborate on that statement?

THE DEFENDANT: There was rioting everywhere—people were just going crazy. We lost—every day, I remember, we lost somebody. John Harriman—my deputy—he was kidnapped and butchered by gang members.

Two cops on patrol—they were just kids, they'd joined up right after the Pulse, wanted to help out—their squad car was firebombed, they roasted in there. God.

MR. BLOOD: So it would be fair to say that there was a great deal of tension between police and the public?

THE DEFENDANT: Some of the public. Most people were happy we were out there defending them. Defending their property.

MR. BLOOD: Very well. I now direct your attention to the events of August 18, 2009. The riots in Gasworks Park.

THE DEFENDANT: I remember.

MR. BLOOD: What do you remember?

THE DEFENDANT: There was a big demonstration down there. I'm sorry—it would be more accurate to say the demonstration started in the financial district that afternoon, and ended up in the park shortly after dark.

MR. BLOOD: Please go on.

THE DEFENDANT: I wasn't actually on duty, so I can only offer you a broad outline of what happened that evening. There were apparently a group of hard-core demonstrators—two or three dozen—who refused to disperse, according to reports from officers on the scene. They actually incited people in the park to attack the officers on crowd control.

MR. BLOOD: And what happened then?

THE DEFENDANT: As I understand it, the officers defended themselves.

MR. BLOOD: They used tear gas. And tasers.

MR. ZACCARO: Objection, Your Honor.

THE COURT: Sustained. Mr. Blood, you're not the one giving testimony.

MR. BLOOD: Chief Miller, how did the officers defend themselves?

THE DEFENDANT: With tear gas. And tasers.

MR. BLOOD: And what happened next?

THE DEFENDANT: Some demonstrators continued to ignore orders to disperse. They continued to assault the officers, physically and verbally.

MR. BLOOD: And then . . .

THE DEFENDANT: Shots were fired. After that, the demonstration broke up.

MR. BLOOD: What happened as a result of those shots?

THE DEFENDANT: Eighteen people died.

MR. BLOOD: Eighteen unarmed protesters.

MR. ZACCARO: Your Honor—

MR. BLOOD: I withdraw that statement. Now, Mr. Miller, can you tell us how you first became aware of the shooting?

THE DEFENDANT: An officer on the scene called me at home. I rushed there at once.

MR. BLOOD: Go on.

THE DEFENDANT: I saw the bodies, and . . . we decided on a cover-up.

MR. BLOOD: We?

THE DEFENDANT: I did—after consulting with the officers on the scene. We decided to move the bodies, and bury them elsewhere.

MR. BLOOD: Sand Point?

THE DEFENDANT: Yes—although first I consulted with—

THE COURT: Let's stay on the topic here, gentlemen. Mr. Blood?

MR. BLOOD: Yes, Your Honor. Mr. Miller, can you tell the court who was involved in the actual shooting?

THE DEFENDANT: You want names?

MR. BLOOD: Yes, sir.

THE DEFENDANT: All right. Sergeant William Benedict. Patrolmen Charles Lota and Richard Greenberg. Donald Gill. Herman Colberg. Ray Saunders. Timothy Carew. Gregory Kilroy. Doug Moller. I think that's everyone.

MR. BLOOD: Thank you, Mr. Miller.

MR. ZACCARO: Your Honor, I'd like it noted that we are now providing the district attorney with a list of the officers involved.

THE COURT: So noted. Does the protectorate have any further questions?

MR. BLOOD: No, Your Honor.

MS. GALNICK: No, sir.

MR. ZACCARO: Your Honor, in light of my client's complete and unconditional cooperation, I'd like to move for an immediate dismissal of the charges against him.

THE COURT: I think such a move would require the concurrence of the protectorate. Ms. Galnick?

MS. GALNICK: At this time, the protectorate is unwilling to make such a concurrence, Your Honor.

THE COURT: Very well. Then—

MR. ZACCARO: If it please the court. My client and I would like a moment to confer.

THE COURT: Very well. The court will take this opportunity to recess. We will return at 10:00 A.M., promptly.

THE CLERK: All rise.

Beginning at 10:00 A.M., approximately.

THE CLERK: Court is in session, case 98-012, Military Protectorate of Seattle versus Rollins A. Miller, the Honorable Judge George Herman Speers presiding.

THE COURT: Chief Miller, I remind you that you are still under oath.

THE DEFENDANT: Yes, sir.

MR. ZACCARO: Counselor, at this time my client would like to offer additional information to the court.

THE COURT: Concerning . . .

MR. ZACCARO: Some related disappearances during the years in question.

THE COURT: Now hold on a minute, Counselor—

MS. GALNICK: Your Honor, this is highly irregular. The protectorate feels strongly that significant consideration due the defendant has already—

THE COURT: There won't be any deals made here without your approval, Ms. Galnick.

THE DEFENDANT: I'm ~~prepared to talk about a lot of things related~~ to the riot squads, Your Honor. The Coffeehouse Crackdown, Sector 55—

THE COURT: Strike that statement from the record!

MR. ZACCARO: Your Honor?

THE COURT: You hear me, clerk? Strike that from the record.

THE CLERK: Yes, sir.

THE DEFENDANT: Judge, you can't—

THE COURT: Don't tell me what I can and cannot do in my courtroom. I tell you we're not going to hear testimony on that subject. And I forbid counsel—under the threat of contempt—to discuss the subject outside this courtroom.

MS. GALNICK: Your Honor, I'm puzzled.

THE COURT: See that you stay that way.

MR. ZACCARO: Your Honor, may I approach the bench?

THE COURT: You stay right where you are, sir. Court is adjourned for the day. We'll pick up tomorrow—testimony will be under seal. Court closed to all but essential personnel. Is that understood, bailiff? Very well. That's all.

THE CLERK: All rise.

Session Ends

SEATTLE
On-Line

The Emerald City's Number One Matchmaking Service!

Today is Wednesday April 17 2021
THE FIRST DAY OF THE REST OF YOUR LIFE!

---

panther 19 (ID=14) citizen k what kind of name is that?

citizenk (ID=54) i'm the orson welles of my time—multitalented and underappreciated

panther 19 (ID=14) wtf?

citizenk (ID=54) never mind panther what's that for

panther 19 (ID=14) i'm slinky

citizenk (ID=54) whoa

iionly (ID=0X) hey is this conversation eyes only or can I cut in?

citizenk (ID=54) don't go anywhere panther I'll be right back

panther 19 (ID=14) who's this? your boyfriend?

citizenk (ID=54) hey. You read the transcript?

iionly (ID=0X) hold on

)(&#KLJSAEF

iionly (ID=0X) all right we're secure. Go ahead.

citizenk (ID=54) so you got the transcript?

iionly (ID=0X) Yeah, thanks. Any way to get inside that courtroom tomorrow?

citizenk (ID=54) Doubtful. Speers wants to approve the list personally. The guy is bent, big-time.

iionly (ID=0X) That's for sure. Wish I knew whose pocket he was in.

citizenk (ID=54) Somebody who doesn't want Miller to testify. My guess is Speers isn't going to let the chief say another word.

iionly (ID=0X) Is the chief in custody now?

citizenk (ID=54) No. He posted bail this afternoon. Two hundred fifty g's.

)(&#KLJSAEF

citizenk (ID=54) He's got bodyguards two huge ex-cops

citizenk (ID=54) hey you there?

citizenk (ID=54) anyone? panther?

METRO EDITION

Seattle Post

THE VOICE OF PUGET SOUND

59 Cents Plus tax

Thursday, April 15, 2021

****

MILLER ASSASSINATED!

Ex-Chief Gunned Down in Broad Daylight

by Brooks Johnson
A Post Exclusive

Only hours after appearing in court on charges related to last week's discovery of a mass grave at Sand Point Naval Base, former Police Chief Rollins Miller was shot to death by an unknown assailant. The incident occurred at 4:10 P.M. Wednesday, just outside his daughter's University Heights residence.

According to witnesses, the shooter—described as an African American man in his midtwenties—avoided capture by escaping into a waiting vehicle. He is still being sought by police.

Miller, whose tenure as Seattle police chief was marked by frequent accusations of brutality and misconduct, appeared to be on his way to jail earlier this week after evidence surfaced connecting him to the bodies discovered at Sand Point. Courtroom sources indicated that Miller and his attorney, Carl Zaccaro Jr., had sought a deal guaranteeing the chief immunity from prosecution, in exchange for providing the names of those involved in the mass execution.

There are also rumors—unconfirmed at this time—that Miller's own death was an execution, intended to prevent the chief from offering that testimony.

Miller, a longtime resident of the Seattle area, first joined the department in 1998 as a detective. Ten years later, he had worked his way into the top position, and was chief in June 2009 when the Pulse struck. When the Military Protectorate of Seattle was established, then–Mayor Beltran confirmed Miller's position and bestowed additional authority on him, unifying the sector police under his command as well.

Miller's wife, Rachel, was a victim of the first wave of riots that came in the wake of the Pulse, and many attribute the chief's inflexible position on demonstrators to that incident. Miller is survived by his children—son Rollins Jr., a businessman in Portland, and daughters Andrea and Karin, both Seattle residents.

Police are urging anyone with information on the

See Miller page 8

We were right back where we started from.

Sanders had led us to Miller. Miller had led us to Sand Point and the eighteen buried bodies. But now Miller was dead, and our investigation into Margaret Curran's disappearance—into the mystery of Sector 55—was dead in the water.

Sure, we knew Speers had covered up Miller's testimony, but getting to him would probably have been just as impossible as getting to Lemkin or Marbury.

One good thing came out of the whole mess—the families of those eighteen people killed by the riot squads back in 2010 finally had some closure. But Asha and I had nothing—except for the Sand Point company info, and Miller's phone records.

I looked those over one more time. All the outside numbers Miller had called back then were now out of service . . . except for one.

DECRYPTION: SECURE 8 DECRYPTION STAMP: 5/8/21 ORIGINAL TRANSCRIPT: 4/15/21 L = Cale, Logan, A = Ames Brothers Phone Operator

FILE BEGINS

A: Ames Brothers Construction. Can I help you?

L: Hello—this is 879-2638-4638?

A: Yes, it is.

L: Good. My name is John Eastman, and I'm wondering if I can ask you a few questions.

A: This is a place of business, sir.

L: I understand that. I'm with the—ah, Greater Seattle Chamber of Commerce. I'll make this very quick.

A: All right.

L: You're a construction company?

A: That's correct. Ames Brothers Construction.

L: And you've been in business about how long?

A: Almost fifty years.

L: Really?

A: That's right. The company was started by John Ames back in the 1970s.

L: And you've had the same phone number all that time?

A: Well. No. The same number since about a year after the Pulse.

L: So since 2010?

A: That's correct.

L: That's what I needed to know. Thank you very much.

A: Say, what's this for?

L: Just a little survey we're conducting on the stability of area businesses. Say, I wonder if you could tell me a little bit about your company? I'm looking to have a little work done on my house.

A: Well, we're a pretty specialized kind of firm.

L: Is that so?

A: Yes. If you have a fax number, I could send you out some information.

FILE CONTINUES

Butch Ames

Ames Brothers Construction

For more than forty years, industry leaders in underground, earth-sheltered designs

Leroy Ames

Thinking of building a new home? Concerned about the environment, about security, about cost-effectiveness? Why not consider an Ames earth-sheltered design? We work with you—from concept to construction—to build your dream house.

John Ames pioneered the concept of the earth-protected environment almost half a century ago—and today, the company he started still sets the standard. Ames Brothers Construction is universally acknowledged as the best in the business, with decades of experience in all facets of the construction process.

SITE SELECTION AND DEVELOPMENT: With over four thousand successful projects to our credit, we've mastered the techniques for excavating and preparing construction areas in all types of terrain—from suburban flatland to virgin mountain forest.

HOME DESIGN: Our on-staff architects work with you to create the blueprint for your home—or bring us your rough sketches, and we'll turn them into reality.

CONSTRUCTION: We use only the finest lumber, concrete (100 percent reinforced, highest-quality rebar), and metals on Ames jobs.

MAINTENANCE AND REPAIR: We stand behind the homes we build, and are available to act as consultants or on-site repair teams. Depending on site location, emergency twenty-four-hour service is also available.

TECHNICAL SERVICES: When customers select Ames, they get its comprehensive technical services, including computerized estimating and cost accounting, guaranteed environmental compliance, and seamless connection of your home to existing utilities and city services.

QUALITY CONTROL AND ASSURANCE: Leroy and Butch Ames are committed to preserving the legacy of quality construction established by their father—no matter how large or small the job.

Come see models of an Ames Earth Home at:
AMES BROTHERS CONSTRUCTION *** 2146 Industrial Parkway *** Tacoma Washington 90949
Or visit us on the Web at www.amesearthhomes.com
Or call 879-AMES-HOME, toll-free!

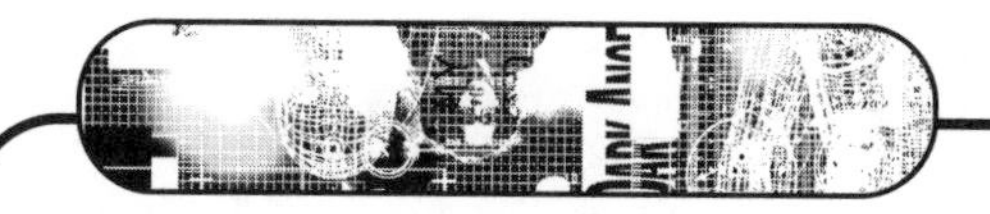

TO: iionly@pfpfree.net

FROM: seb2009@pfpfree.net

DATE: 4/15/21

RE: Ames Brothers Construction

You're right, there's something odd about this company.

Up until 2014 they were a relatively small concern—never more than a dozen employees, never more than a million gross annually. Then in late 2014, they got a major influx of cash—ten million dollars, according to their accounts—and dropped half of it on new equipment. German stuff, nothing but the best. They took on two dozen new hires—all of them Chinese nationals with temporary work permits—and finished up all their existing contracts within a few weeks.

Then they disappeared off the face of the earth. For a period of six months, from November 2014 through April 2015, there aren't any work records, any bank records, anything at all related to Ames Brothers Construction.

Judging from the phone records, this is the same time period during which Miller was calling them frequently—at least once a week. Often right after he spoke to Sand Point.

Obviously Ames Construction was working for Miller. Not Miller-the-police-chief, but Miller the operations manager for Sand Point Redevelopment. What they were doing for him, though . . .

That's the sixty-four-thousand-dollar question, as they used to say.

We were able to find out a little more about Ames Construction—specifically, John Ames, the company's founder. He retired in 2015, and moved to Barbados—where he's apparently living like a king.

It was a safe bet that Ames's 401(k) came courtesy of Sand Point Redevelopment. The question we couldn't answer, though, was what he'd done to earn it. I spent hours scouring the Net for a connection between Ames and Margaret Curran, between Miller and Curran, between Lemkin and Marbury and anything at all to do with a Sector 55.

About midnight I gave up and went for a walk downtown to clear my head. It's pretty desolate down there these days. All the old tourist attractions—places that used to be lit up in neon till two in the morning—got trashed in the first few years of rioting after the Pulse. I remembered them like they used to be—Pike Place, the Space Needle, Pioneer Square . . .

And bingo—a little lightbulb went off in my head. A little purple lightbulb.

TAKE JOE MORGAN'S TOUR OF UNDERGROUND SEATTLE AND SEE THE CITY AS IT WAS A HUNDRED YEARS AGO!

Tired of your run-of-the-mill tourist attractions?
Want to do something a little out of the ordinary?
WHY NOT TAKE A TRIP BACK IN TIME?

Experience Joe Morgan's world-famous tour of underground Seattle, and you'll make memories that will last you a lifetime!

Underneath the bustling streets of Seattle's Pioneer Square lie remnants of a lost world—entire city blocks of the Emerald City, virtually untouched since the nineteenth century!

Underground Seattle owes its existence to the Great Fire of 1889, which destroyed the entire city in less than twelve hours! When rebuilding began, city leaders decided to avoid the frequent flooding that had plagued their city, by raising the streets up a full story. Iron beams were laid, and new roads built on top of them. But the old streets—and the storefronts that had lined them—remained in place underneath, undisturbed for decades.

For a time, people were well aware of the history that lay buried just beneath their feet. Many building owners, in fact, used their old street-level stores as storage areas. The city encouraged this practice by embedding thick glass windowpanes in the concrete of the new sidewalks, to allow light to shine through. Some of the glass was tinted purple, which made for a memorable light show underground.

But as time passed, memories faded—until by the middle of the twentieth century underground Seattle lay abandoned, all but forgotten by the city—and the world.

But no longer.

Now all it takes is a trip down a short flight of stairs for you to visit that long-buried past—to catch a glimpse of life at the turn of the last century.

Make historic Seattle part of your future . . .
Get tickets for Joe Morgan's Underground Seattle today!

Tours are approximately forty-five minutes in length. They begin hourly at 9:00 A.M. from Dusty Sparkler's Tavern and continue until 6:00 P.M. Afternoon and evening customers receive one free cocktail of their choice (top-shelf drinks $2 extra). All visitors receive a piece of souvenir sidewalk glass, and a fifteen-minute slide show featuring scenes from Seattle's past and *Kolchak: The Night Stalker*!

Call 1-800-JOE'S-TOUR Now and Make Your Reservations!

I took that tour when I was a kid. I remember going down a flight of stairs, and suddenly there were all these dusty old streets and storefronts looking like pages out of a history book. There's a lot more down there than most people realize.

And I also remember looking up through the glass sidewalks, with the light shining down through them. It was purple, Matt. The light was purple. Just like Margaret said in her note.

It didn't prove she was down there, of course. But it was a step forward.

I went back to the apartment and called Asha. She reminded me that underground Seattle's been closed off for years—that nobody's allowed down there anymore, ever since the riots in 2014. The Coffeehouse Crackdowns.

"We'll have to be careful, going in," she said.

A lot of things suddenly fell into place for me. Ames Construction, for one—they'd worked for Miller during that same time period, 2014, 2015, when the underground was first closed off. Building something for the chief, and his friends at Sand Point.

What if that something was the prison where Margaret was begin held? What if Sector 55 referred to that facility as well? After all, downtown was Sector 5. Sector 55 might refer to the area underneath that.

It was a lot to assume.

But that morning, I was eager to get out there, and prove—or disprove—my theory.

It was April 18.

That night, my EYES ONLY hack was traced. I was lucky to escape with my life.

Since then, I've been unable to contact Curran's daughter Asha. Unable to follow up on any of this.

That's where you come in.

Go to underground Seattle. Find out what's down there now.

Find Margaret Curran.

The Phoenix Project

Crossfile:

Donald Lydecker

Manticore

Mediterranean Coalition

Pope Leo XVI

THE PHOENIX PROJECT

DECEMBER 31, 2019/JANUARY 7, 2020

SPECIAL DOUBLE ISSUE

MAN OF THE YEAR: POPE LEO XVI

HARDCOPY

BORN AGAIN:
The Church Takes Back
the High Moral Ground

www.hardcopymagazine.com MC Keyword: Hardcopy

B Y   K E I T H   F R E E D

THE NEW MILLENNIUM WAS SUPPOSED TO BE MORE OF THE SAME. America ascendant, growing ever more powerful—with the rest of the world bowing obsequiously and following wherever the red, white and blue wanted to lead them.

But a funny thing happened on the way to the second American Century. A thing called the Pulse—a nuclear bomb that fried every computer east of the Rocky Mountains, and transformed the U.S.A. into just another debtor nation, trying to make ends meet.

What people didn't immediately realize was that the Pulse did a lot more than mortally wound the American economy. It left a hole at the top of the geopolitical food chain that threatened to plunge civilization itself into chaos.

It may sound like exaggeration, but consider events on the world stage, post-Pulse:

". . . the Roman Catholic Church is not only the spiritual center of the civilized world, but its conscience as well . . ."

2010: China seizes Taiwan, nationalizes its industries, and expels all foreigners. The newly united country is, in turn, expelled from the United Nations. Within a few short months, repercussions from that action effectively mark the end of the U.N., on the eve of its sixty-third birthday.

2011: Israel tightens its grip on the Syrian territories, and in December goes to war with the Arab League. Increased terrorist activity in the region causes France and Italy—along with fourteen other nations—to join forces with Greater Israel to form the Mediterranean Coalition.

That same year, India and Pakistan engage in not one, but two all-out wars over Kashmir, leaving hundreds of millions dead. Biological weapons are used on a massive scale, leading neighboring countries to ban all travel—including airline flights—in and out of the region.

And that's just the short list. It doesn't include the riots in Medina, the invasion of El Salvador, the war in Ukraine, or half a dozen other regional conflicts.

By 2017, observers saw in these battles the seeds of World War III—and were predicting such a conflict within the next half a dozen years. With the world's former policemen—the U.N. and the U.S.A.—effectively sidelined, war, it seemed, might become a permanent state of affairs.

Then in November 2017, Roberto Perez—at that time Cardinal Perez of Portugal—was chosen as the 265th head of the Catholic Church. The new pope became the first man from his country in close to eight hundred years to achieve such an honor, but Perez's assumption of the title—he officially became Pope Leo XVI in January 2018—merited relatively little attention from the global media.

Not surprising, perhaps, considering how out of touch the church seemed to be with twenty-first-century society. Many of Leo's predecessors, no matter how great their personal popularity, had been ineffective actors on the global stage. Most observers felt that no matter who was in residence at the Vatican, the papacy itself no longer had a part to play in world affairs.

What those observers failed to take into account, however, was Christianity's continuing hold on the hearts—and minds—of billions of people worldwide. The message—if not the messengers—remained a powerful force for unity. The religion itself, in fact, was the fastest growing on the planet, its followers a potential army—awaiting only a commander capable of rallying them.

Leo XVI, as it turned out, was precisely the man for the job.

Within months of assuming the papacy, he issued his first formal encyclical—the Kent Proclamations, as they have come to be known—which called for an end to some of the church's most hallowed traditions. Those traditions, many felt, had erected an unnatural wall between church leaders and their flock, rendering them ineffective figureheads. Enforced celibacy, sexual discrimination, and even papal infallibility were all addressed within this historic document. Leo—a youthful, dynamic figure—instantly became the most popular pope in centuries, and he soon began wielding that popularity in ways no one could have envisioned.

In July 2018, he visited Korea, and spoke directly via satellite linkup to the young people of neighboring China, urging them to end the occupation of Taiwan and abandon their Communist leaders. Two weeks later, he broadcast much the same message from Japan.

That November, during a visit to the Archbishop of Canterbury, he urged closer ties between the Church of England and Rome. He made similar overtures during later talks with representatives of the Greek and Russian Orthodox Churches.

In August 2019, taking perhaps his most controversial stand, he addressed the Italian parliament and urged them to repeal that country's membership in the Mediterranean Coalition. Condemning the coalition as "morally bankrupt," he urged his fellow Italians to abide by the principles of democracy and forgo the use of war as an instrument of policy.

Gradually, Leo's representatives—the cardinals and bishops, priests and nuns—began to imitate his forthrightness, and speak their own minds. Today, for the first time in recorded history, it seems safe to say that the Roman Catholic Church is not only the spiritual center of the civilized world, but its conscience as well. And with Leo firmly in charge, the Vatican seems certain to continue on that course.

Next year, in fact, despite widespread demands asking Catholics to abide by the constitutional separation of church and state, the pope is planning his first trip to the United States of America, where he is expected to speak out on a wide variety of issues.

I don't care if you're religious or not—that article should prove something to you.

One man really can make a difference in the world. For those of us raised in the shadow of the church's endless scandals at the turn of the century, it may be hard to believe that the one man was the pope. But what Leo achieved in his first two years as pontiff was just astounding.

Unfortunately, those first two years were all he got.

POPE ASSASSINATED

The London World-Times

80P Newspaper of the Year No. 987 Friday December 25 2020 www.timesonline.co.uk

Leo XVI Shot During Mass

World Watches in Horror

College of Cardinals to Convene Immediately on Successor

By Richard McGrory in London and Graham Mastrangelo in Rome

In the end, even the best security money could buy was not enough.

Pope Leo XVI, probably the most popular and controversial figure of the new millennium, and the subject of countless death threats since his assumption of the papacy two years ago, was assassinated last night as he presided over midnight mass in St. Peter's Basilica. A single shot fired from high above the papal altar struck the pope at 1:04 A.M. local time, killing him instantly. Catholics around the world, watching the service via satellite television, witnesssed the horrible scene.

According to preliminary reports, the as-yet-unidentified killer had posed as one of the *sampietrini*—"the men of St. Peter," workers who maintain the basilica's interior and exterior—in order to gain entrance to the cathedral. He then joined a team of Vatican security personnel posted in the shadows of the *baldachino*—the ninety-five-foot bronze canopy that looms above the floor of the basilica.

At some point after the mass had begun, the killer murdered the security guard nearest him, then used the guard's weapon to assassinate the pope—after which he made an extraordinary attempt, called "superhuman" according to several witnesses, at escaping the dozens of security personnel and *polizei* who converged on his position.

Then, in a second shocking display of violence, when his capture seemed inevitable, the man literally blew himself apart in midair, apparently triggering an explosive device wired to his body.

Inspector Carlo Nestor, the Vatican director of public security, promised that his department would identify the gunman and pursue "without mercy" any other who may have been involved in the shooting.

"We will find out who was responsible for this awful tragedy," Nestor told a hastily assembled group of broadca[illegible] and journalists.

The assassination took place a [illegible] before the pope's departure for Am[illegible] where he was expected to meet bot[illegible] President Tolbert and Presiden[illegible] Beekman on a number of issues, i[illegible] ing the recent tragic death of [illegible] Ruiz in El Salvador, and the cont[illegible] American military presence ther[illegible] sions between the Vatican and the [illegible] have been increasing as of lat[illegible]

Turn to page 3A, column 1

In retrospect, the press had it right. Leo's death was hardly surprising. All the enemies he made, the way he refused to negotiate on what he considered "matters of conscience"—it's no wonder someone took him out.

The question, obviously, was who. It wasn't the kind of thing EYES ONLY would normally look into.

But then again . . .

Leo wasn't the normal sort of pope.

TO: <Recipient list>

FROM: iionly@pfpfree.net

DATE: 12/28/20

RE: Pope Leo

I want to know what happened here—who this shooter was, how he managed to infiltrate the sampietrini, if he was a lone gunman or working for someone else, anything. Everything.

Anyone?

TO: iionly@pfpfree.net

FROM: gatekeeper@pfpfree.net

DATE: 12/28/20

RE: Pope Leo

Nada. But I can tell you some people here aren't upset in the least by what happened—Leo was a squeaky wheel, and they're glad for a little quiet.

TO: iionly@pfpfree.net

FROM: troy22@pfpfree.net

DATE: 12/28/20

RE: Pope Leo

I might be able to access some related intel. Senate Foreign Affairs Subcommittee has been holding hearings on his upcoming visit.

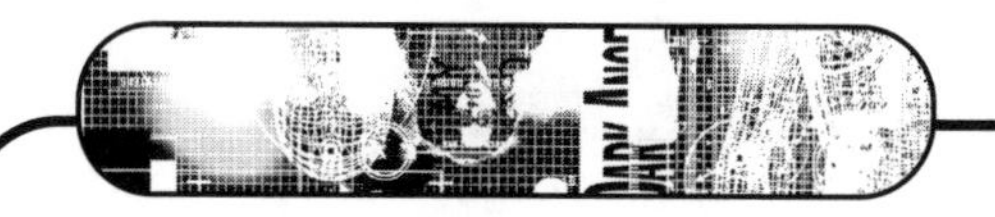

TO: troy22@pfpfree.net

FROM: iionly@pfpfree.net

DATE: 12/29/20

RE: Pope Leo

Can you get transcripts?

TO: iionly@pfpfree.net

FROM: troy22@pfpfree.net

DATE: 12/28/20

RE: Pope Leo

That's what I'm talking about. The hearings are closed to the public, though, and my source on the Congressional Data Network is out of town during the recess. She's due back in ten days—I'll keep you posted.

TO: iionly@pfpfree.net

FROM: thecolonel@pfpfree.net

DATE: 12/30/20

RE: Pope Leo

Nothing on the shooting. News of another kind, though: I'm being transferred. I'll contact you again when I can.

TO: iionly@pfpfree.net

FROM: gatekeeper@pfpfree.net

DATE: 1/6/21

RE: <no subject was specified>

Something really strange happened yesterday.

Late morning, a tech guy comes in, says he's got to "optimize file cluster allocation" on our servers. Said someone in the department had complained about a significant lag time in retrieving case records.

I hadn't noticed anything, but . . . whatever.

What I did notice was that this guy wasn't from the regular tech company. And that he spent two hours installing new software onto the servers, instead of using the programs we already had.

Now, you know me—I don't trust techs. I've got a firewall—my own design, thank you very much—in place on my system to prevent anything from infecting it.

Two hours after this "tech" leaves, alerts start flashing all over my screen. Intrusion detected, intrusion detected, file alteration in progress yada yada. Bastard put a virus into the system. It was trying to access my computer via the network connection. Spent the better part of that afternoon extracting the code.

It was expert stuff. I'll spare you the tech talk, but in a nutshell, the virus was looking for files containing a specific alphanumeric string. Whenever it found that string, it was designed to erase it, and delete all associated files.

What makes this interesting is the string itself:

9843092ZEDA990389200CK.

Looks like gobbledygook to the average citizen, but not to me. I see that number, and I think: passport I.D.

I couldn't find anything on the string in my system, and I knew the virus had already deleted it from our servers.

But that's why you always back up your work, right?

Our servers back up to a secure facility in Land's End, Pennsylvania. I had somebody there run a search on the string immediately, before they got a "tech call" of their own. Turned up a hit—the passport with that number belongs to one Brian Pollack, of Cincinnati, Ohio. Sergeant Brian Pollack, U.S. Marine

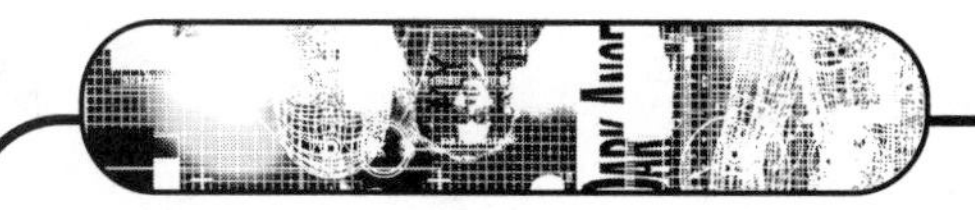

Corps. I should say belonged, actually, because Pollack's military records list him as KIA, June 4, 2010, in Iraq.

Something funny going on here, Chief.

TO: iionly@pfpfree.net

FROM: frequentflyer@pfpfree.net

DATE: 1/17/21

RE: Pollack

Funny is one word for it, all right.

Records show a Sergeant Brian Pollack boarded a C-141 military transport on August 5 last year, out of McChord AFB, destination LIRG.

Nothing further available on that flight—classified top secret, Eyes Only (no pun intended).

Here's something else.

LIRG is the airport code for Guidonia—a military base just outside of Rome.

TO: iionly@pfpfree.net

FROM: thecolonel@pfpfree.net

DATE: 1/17/21

RE: Pollack

En route to my new assignment, can't help much at the moment. But . . .

Reusing passport I.D.'s, military serial numbers, etc., FYI, is SOP on covert operations.

Food for thought.

Food for thought indeed.

I was starting to get a bad feeling about this. An Iran-Contra, Hussein-Castro, black ops kind of feeling. A feeling like the decision to kill the pope might have been made right here, in the old U.S. of A.

It was just a feeling, of course. I still needed facts to confirm it. Facts about covert U.S. operations—past, present, and future. DoD and NSA position papers. U.S. Army troop movements, unscheduled resupply operations—I had to start with some very broad brushstrokes. It was a lot to ask for.

As a certain someone was quick to remind me.

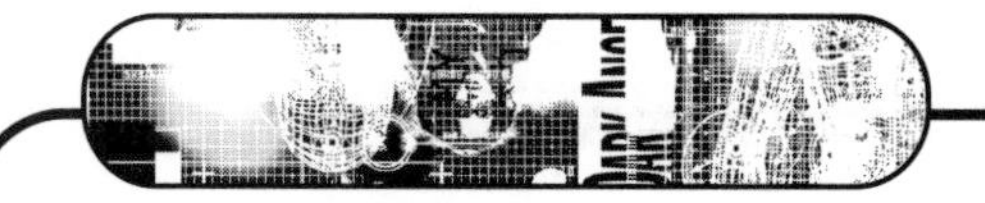

TO: iionly@pfpfree.net

FROM: deweyd@pfpfree.net

DATE: 1/16/21

RE: A little help

Always happy to help EYES ONLY. But those search parameters you gave me are too broad, especially for documents that haven't been declassified yet. The query will take several minutes to run, and somebody's bound to notice.

Can you narrow it down?

TO: deweyd@pfpfree.net

FROM: iionly@pfpfree.net

DATE: 1/16/21

RE: A little help

Add the following operators:

Guidonia

Brian Michael Pollack

TO: iionly@pfpfree.net

FROM: deweyd@pfpfree.net

DATE: 1/16/21

RE: A little help

Nothing.

TO: deweyd@pfpfree.net

FROM: iionly@pfpfree.net

DATE: 1/16/21

RE: A little help

Add:

Papal Visit United States

Greater Israel

Mediterranean Coalition

TO: iionly@pfpfree.net

FROM: deweyd@pfpfree.net

DATE: 1/16/21

RE: A little help

Nothing on the first two.

On number three . . .

Bingo.

DOCUMENT A-21

DoD SPECIAL OPERATIONS

21 April 2020

General Avram Rose
Commander in Chief
United States Army Forces
Mediterranean Theater

1. On or before 5 August 2020, Arizona unit will arrive Rome Italy, in furtherance of Phoenix objectives. Operational command of these units will reside in accompanying special ops squadron leader. The purpose of this missive is to inform you that U.S. Army units may be called on for assistance.

2. In reference to our meeting of 12 December 2019, please continue to update this office of on-site tactical situation. Should additional personnel be required, they will arrive at least sixty days in advance of the scheduled operation.

3. Dissemination of any and all information concerning the use of Arizona is reserved to the committee. No other communiqués on the subject or informal releases of information will be permitted.

4. The foregoing directive is issued to you at the direction and with approval of the committee. It is desired that you personally deliver one copy of this directive to the office of the CINC Mediterranean Coalition.

Stendahl

Arizona Unit. Phoenix objectives.

I had no idea what this Stendahl was referring to, but the memo had Arizona flying into Rome on August 5—the same day that "Pollack" arrived. Could be one and the same flight.

It was also clear that the Mediterranean Coalition was somehow involved. If anyone had reason to want Leo out of the picture, it was them.

That bad feeling I had before was only getting stronger.

And then it became a certainty.

TO: iionly@pfpfree.net

FROM: raven@pfpfree.net

DATE: 1/22/21

RE: <no subject was specified>

You're not going to believe this.

I have a friend working forensics over in Italy—he was called in last week by his boss and told he was being loaned out to another department. That other department turned out to be the Inspectorate of Public Security for the Vatican. They wanted my friend to be part of the team they were setting up to identify the assassin, using his DNA.

Yesterday, as he was heading out the door to start work for them, he got a call telling him not to bother to show.

Seems they lost all the DNA samples.

Nobody can be that stupid—can they?

TO: <Recipient list >

FROM: iionly@pfpfree.net

DATE: 1/23/21

RE: <no subject was specified>

See Raven's e-mail, people. Nobody can be that stupid—except on purpose. Somebody didn't want those samples identified. Somebody with a very, very long arm.

We are officially treading in dangerous waters now, everyone. Stay alert.

TO: iionly@pfpfree.net

FROM: deweyd@pfpfree.net

DATE: 1/18/21

RE: A little help

You've got to be kidding. Run a search in the archives for the word "Committee"? Even in connection with the other operands, I'll get millions of hits.

TO: deweyd@pfpfree.net

FROM: iionly@pfpfree.net

DATE: 1/18/21

RE: A little help

Take the weekend.

TO: iionly@pfpfree.net

FROM: deweyd@pfpfree.net

DATE: 1/18/21

RE: A little help

Ha ha.

No way I am putting that word into the query form. I will try the others for you—but I'll also take your advice about the weekend. I'm hitting a lot of classified servers—DoD, Homeland Security, Congressional Archives—running these queries. Makes me nervous doing it during business hours.

TO: iionly@pfpfree.net

FROM: deweyd@pfpfree.net

DATE: 1/20/21

RE: My search . . .

. . . returned twenty-seven results.

Number six is the one you're looking for. An internal DoD memorandum outlining the basis for a major new foreign policy . . .

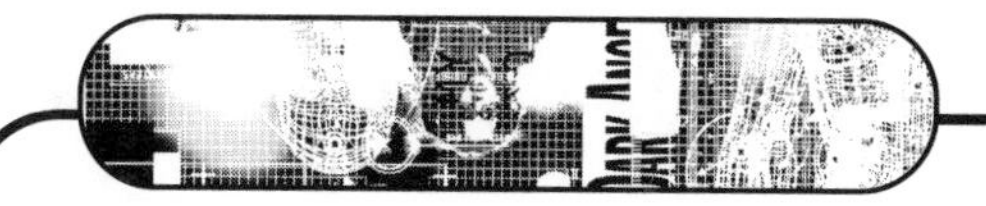

Code name: The Phoenix Project.

Downloading all the info now—you'll have it shortly.

TO: deweyd@pfpfree.net

FROM: iionly@pfpfree.net

DATE: 1/21/21

RE: The weekend

Your idea of shortly and mine vary greatly.

I'm still waiting on those documents.

TO: deweyd@pfpfree.net

FROM: iionly@pfpfree.net

DATE: 1/22/21

RE: Weekend

Any news?

TO: iionly@pfpfree.net

FROM: asherman@pfpfree.net

DATE: 1/22/21

RE: Dewey

You'll want to see this.

Picked it up off the wire services.

Librarian Murdered

Washington, D.C., January 21
(Wire Services)

The body of Carl Rhodes, a Library of Congress researcher, was found stabbed to death in an alleyway one block from his apartment late Sunday evening. Police say the body may have lain undiscovered for as long as two days.

Rhodes, a Georgetown resident, was forty-two years old. He had worked for the Library of Congress for the last twelve years. Prior to that, he was a graduate teaching assistant at the Yale School of Journalism in New Haven, Connecticut.

Coworkers recalled Rhodes's devotion to his job, and his eagerness to share his expertise with colleagues and private researchers.

"If any of us had a question on where to find something, he could answer right off the top of his head," said Ivica Cassel, who worked in the office next to Rhodes for the last two years. "The Library system, the Cutter system, the Dewey Decimal system—he had all of them memorized."

Authorities are asking anyone with information on the crime to contact them.

TO: iionly@pfpfree.net

FROM: troy22@pfpfree.net

DATE: 1/24/21

RE: Deweyd

Funeral sucked.

I'm sorry, I know I'm not supposed to say that. But I couldn't focus on feeling sad. I was too scared. Thought whoever killed him—cops still have nothing, and they never will—might be there too, looking for other targets.

I don't know—these last few days, I feel like somebody's looking over my shoulder. And every time I turn around, I expect to see them standing right there with a gun and a badge—or maybe just a gun.

I can't do this anymore. I need to take a break for a while.

I'm sorry.

TO: troy22@pfpfree.net

FROM: iionly@pfpfree.net

DATE: 1/24/21

RE: Deweyd

Take whatever time you need—and thanks for everything. I'll expect a list of your sources via the usual method.

TO: iionly@pfpfree.net

FROM: gatekeeper@pfpfree.net

DATE: 1/25/21

RE: Deweyd

My turn to pose as a tech guy.

Got into Dewey's office yesterday afternoon, pretending to do a little maintenance on the archives we keep over at the library. Not such a stretch, really—I have been over there before. And don't worry—I was very careful.

His hard drive had already been wiped—no surprise there. Thought there might be a way to recover some of the info, so I popped in a replacement and slipped the original out with me.

Took a few hours, but I think I found what we were looking for. It's a mission statement, believe it or not. Attached.

DEPARTMENT OF DEFENSE

TOP SECRET

MEMORANDUM

DECLASSIFIED

THE PHOENIX PROJECT

January 12, 2015

The Phoenix project seeks a rechanneling of government resources and individual energies toward a single goal: the restoration of America as a superpower, based on the contention that the spread of American values and the American democratic impulse was a progressive force throughout the world.

Furthermore, had this force not been halted in its tracks by the events of June 9, 2009, we believe that by midcentury a truly representative world government would have come into being, one that would fairly reflect the hopes and aspirations of the greater family of nations.

It is toward the resumption of that process that we propose the following substantive shift in American foreign policy.

By its nature, Phoenix must necessarily be a covert undertaking. However, in the furtherance of its overall goals, Phoenix can utilize both overt and covert means, as outlined below.

Overt Components:

The thrust of existing foreign propaganda should be altered to emphasize America's historical successes in the relevant theater of operations (Appendix A).

The thrust of existing foreign aid should be rechanneled to solely pro-American forces, whether or not those forces are currently in power (Appendix B).

Because the perception of power is sometimes as important as its actual possession, existing military forces should be redeployed to areas where they can make immediate, significant impact (Appendix C).

Alliances with governments antagonistic to the goals of Phoenix—no matter the short-term economic or political benefits—are to be avoided. Alliances will be sought out with governments that can directly aid the furtherance of Phoenix (Appendix D).

Covert Components:

The post-Pulse world resembles in many ways the post-WWII Cold War period, when the two superpowers—the U.S. and the U.S.S.R.—fought a struggle for world domination through proxies, or client nations. This period is correctly recognized by historians today as an apocalyptic struggle between good and evil.

A struggle of the same kind is being played out today on the world stage, though the struggle this time is not between two countries, but between two different ways of life. Between the civilized world, and the uncivilized. Between the forces of order, and those of chaos. And as in the past, we must not shy from utilizing whatever methods necessary—whatever proxies necessary—to achieve our goals.

These methods can include:

Proxy corporations, following economic policies constructive to Phoenix. Funding to allow the pursuit of otherwise nonprofitable activities can be sought from private and government ("off the books") sources (Appendix E).

Proxy armies, either state-affiliated or "black ops," in pursuit of targets actively hostile to Phoenix. Along these lines, DoD has developed a highly versatile weapon—a twenty-first-century soldier that can be utilized in either deep-cover situations (assassination) or field operations (combat scenarios). In either case, training and unit capabilities will both prevent exposure and keep casualties to a minimum. The flexibility that these new units provide us cannot be overemphasized: in cases where we previously might send a thousand soldiers into battle and expect to lose a hundred, we will now be able to send in ten and sustain no casualties (Appendix F).

In conclusion, we believe that when America is strong, the world is safe. When America is able to act unilaterally, free from the constraints imposed on her by a commingling of contradictory impulses from nation-states with differing interests, the world is safe. The image of the Phoenix, rising from the ashes, is the symbol for our project. America, rising from the ashes of the Pulse, to reclaim her place in the world.

Appendixes A–F attached, along with concluding remarks.

Respectfully submitted,

D. Stendahl

This paper was prepared at the direction of the Committee. In addition to the author, valuable input was given by:
Carl Buchanan and Paul Charvel, Department of Homeland Security
George Carson, Department of Defense
John Michael Lodge, Byrd Center for International Relations
Frank Sandoval, Special Liaison
Major General Tai Sunabadum, USAF

Nothing dies as hard as a dream. And the dream shared at heart by every American, ever since the days of Jefferson and Jackson, Lincoln and Grant, Roosevelt and Truman, has been a simple one.

The dream of Manifest Destiny—one nation, under God, destined to rule the world.

People in Washington dreamed that dream more than anyone: they longed for the days when America would speak, and other countries would hurry to obey.

Stendahl had promised them those days back again—and more. No doubt the government had given him what he'd asked for. A fully funded Phoenix Project, in all its overt—and covert—glory.

But Phoenix wasn't just about the good old days. Phoenix was also about the new, twenty-first-century soldier—an extremely powerful weapon, according to Stendahl's memo; so powerful, in fact, that ten of them could take the place of a thousand ordinary men in battle.

A highly versatile weapon capable of being utilized in deep-cover situations as well as in the field. In covert operations—such as assassination. An almost superhuman weapon—one whose capabilities were almost limitless.

Stendahl's paper didn't mention where these twenty-first-century soldiers were supposed to come from. But that was all right. I already knew the answer to that question.

They came from a test tube.

They came from Manticore.

SOURCE: F:/TEMPFILES/NET/EYESONLY/ENGLISH/09282020/TEXT

IMAGES:

. . . /09282020/IMAGES/DODFRM.1

. . . /09282020/IMAGES/DODFRM.2

. . . /09282020/IMAGES/DODFRM.3

. . . /09282020/IMAGES/DODFRM.4

. . . /09282020/IMAGES/DNA.QT

. . . /09282020/IMAGES/FETUS.QT

. . . /09282020/IMAGES/BARRACKS.AVI

. . . /09282020/IMAGES/GILLETE.3

RUN EYES ONLY INTRO

Do not attempt to adjust your set. This is a Streaming Freedom Video bulletin. The cable hack will last exactly sixty seconds. It cannot be traced. It cannot be stopped. And it is the only free voice left in this city.

Since the early 1990s, billions of your tax dollars have been diverted from legitimate government programs in order to fund secret experiments in genetic engineering. This covert operation is known as Project Manticore. Its goal: to create the perfect soldier. Manticore uses recombinant DNA technology to manipulate the human genome. Genetically enhanced for superior strength and speed, these children are held against their will and subjected to relentless training and propaganda. In the fall of 2009, twelve of them escaped from this facility in Gillette, Wyoming.

Manticore spent the next ten years hunting them down, desperate to keep its existence a secret. Some of them were caught, some of them were murdered. Some gave their lives fighting to stay free.

Since these cable hacks began, Manticore has consolidated its operations to a secret location. But they can't hide forever. EYES ONLY will find it. And the people responsible for these crimes will be brought to justice.

BROADCAST DATE: 09/28/20

TIME: 19:10

I broadcast that hack nine months ago. Now it seems prescient. We did find Manticore, and expose it to the world.

The people in charge responded by burning down the facility and trying to destroy the proof of its existence—all the transgenics inside. Living, breathing people who were treated like matériel, to be discarded when their usefulness had ended. Max and I helped them escape.

With their facility trashed, and their perfect soldiers scattered, we figured Manticore was finished. But now it seemed as if we might have been wrong.

Manticore burned down September 2020. The pope was killed three months later. And his killer sure as hell looked like an X5. One of Max's "brothers."

Were some of those soldiers still out there? If so, who was giving them their orders? Somebody high up in the government, that was for certain. Troy had promised me minutes from the closed Senate hearings on Leo's visit. He was gone now—but I still wanted to see them. So I had to go directly to the source.

DECRYPTION: SECURE 9 DECRYPTION STAMP: 5/8/21 ORIGINAL TRANSCRIPT: 2/14/21 L = Cale, Logan, S = *********

FILE BEGINS

S: Senator *****'s office.

L: Is this *****?

S: Yes. Who's calling, please?

L: This is Troy's friend.

S: Oh.

L: Don't say my name.

S: All right.

L: I need your help, *******. Can you talk freely?

S: I don't know if I want to do this.

L: People have died. You can help prevent that from happening again.

S: Or I could be next.

L: That's always a possibility—but that doesn't alter the fact that I need your help, if the truth is to be revealed. If those death are to mean anything.

S: You're so reassuring.

L: So I've been told.

S: All right, I'll help.

L: Thank you, *****.

S: But I can't get the transcripts of those hearings. They've changed access protocols.

L: What about an agenda—a list of witnesses?

S: No. Same thing. Although . . .

L: What?

S: The senator held some private sessions after the hearings—in his office. There may be a record of those on his computer.

FILE CONTINUES

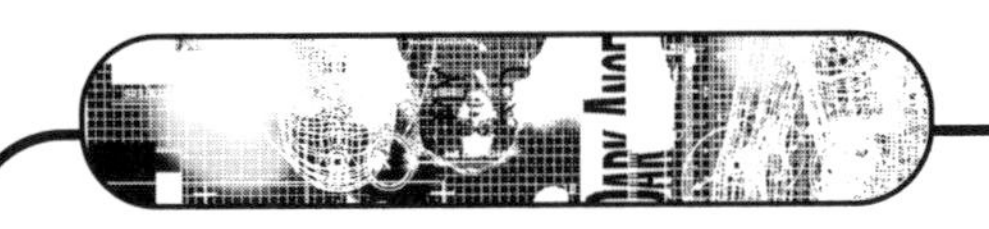

TO: dazzler@pfpfree.net

FROM: iionly@pfpfree.net

DATE: 2/15/21

RE: <no subject was specified>

Dazzler it is. Welcome to the EYES ONLY Informant Net.

I'll look forward to receiving those files.

TO: iionly@pfpfree.net

FROM: dazzler@pfpfree.net

DATE: 2/15/21

RE: Files

All right, here we go. Session transcripts attached.

I have now officially broken the law.

TO: dazzler@pfpfree.net

FROM: iionly@pfpfree.net

DATE: 2/15/21

RE: Files

No, officially you broke the law when you copied them.

Now you've broken several laws.

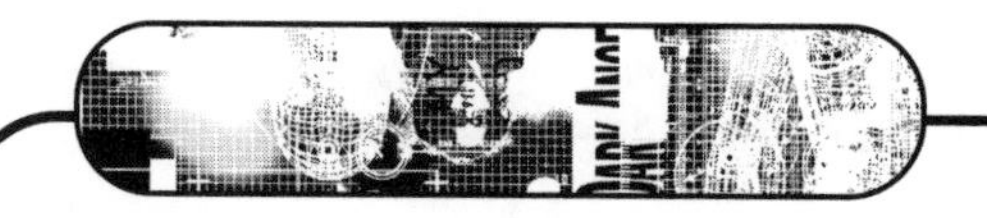

TO: iionly@pfpfree.net

FROM: dazzler@pfpfree.net

DATE: 2/15/21

RE: Files

Mom would be so proud.

TO: dazzler@pfpfree.net

FROM: iionly@pfpfree.net

DATE: 2/15/21

RE: Files

I think she would, actually.

I'll be in touch.

TRANSCRIPT: POST-HEARING SESSION IN SENATOR ****'S OFFICE RE: PAPAL VISIT

April 12, 2020
7:10 p.m.

Senator****:	I don't care if he's carrying a message straight from the Almighty's hands, we are not going to give this man free rein to incite a riot in my state, gentlemen. I can assure you of that.
Undersecretary Myers:	The administration appreciates your position, sir, but you have to recognize that our hands are tied here. The invitation was a private one, the pope accepted it, and we cannot rescind it.
Senator****:	You could exert pressure on the VFW. Make them un-invite him.
Mr. Stendahl:	At which point the press would get hold of it, and the situation would blow up in our faces. No, best to let him speak in Charleston, and deal with the consequences as best we can.
Senator****:	Rolling over, and playing dead. I don't like it, gentlemen.
Undersecretary Myers:	The president does plan on a frank exchange of views with the pope, both before his arrival and during his visit.
Senator****:	Let me remind you, Mr. Myers, you've got an election coming up. There's no guarantee your man is going to be in office when the pope gets here.
Mr. Stendahl:	Mr. Myers—if I may?
Undersecretary Myers:	Go ahead.

Mr. Stendahl: I've talked to Governor Beekman's representatives, and to the governor himself concerning this issue. And I can assure you we're all on the same page here. There is a consensus on our objectives, as outlined by Phoenix, and a consensus on the methods we'll use to achieve those objectives.

Senator****: Well that's good news. Good news indeed.

Speaker (?): Should that man be recording this?

Senator****: These notes are for my private records, sir.

Speaker (?): It's not prudent.

Senator****: I'd ask the colonel to remember that this is my office, and I'll decide what's prudent here.

Mr. Stendahl: The colonel's concern is understandable, Senator. His men are at the forefront of Phoenix—they'll be the ones at risk if the project is exposed.

Senator****: Men. That's not exactly right—is it colonel? These ex fivers?

Speaker (?): X5R, Senator. No, they're not exactly men, sir—or women for that matter. But I'd ask you to remember that they, too, will be putting their lives at risk to achieve your goals. I think they're owed a little respect for that—a little consideration.

Senator****: I take your point.

Speaker (?): Thank you, Senator.

Mr. Stendahl: I suggest we break for dinner and return.

TO: iionly@pfpfree.net

FROM: dazzler@pfpfree.net

DATE: 2/17/21

RE: Participants

Myers is John Myers, fifty-eight years old, Washington, D.C., resident, confirmed bachelor. He was undersecretary of Homeland Security in both the James and Tolbert administrations—he's now a consultant to Boeing/Marbury Aerospace.

Stendahl, I'm having trouble tracking down. There's a David Stendahl in State Department who was briefly ambassador to El Salvador, before the invasion, but he retired a few years ago.

Speaker (?) is obviously military, but no colonels were on the committee witness list that week. There's no way to I.D. him.

TO: dazzler@pfpfree.net

FROM: iionly@pfpfree.net

DATE: 2/17/21

RE: Participants

Thanks. Keep looking into Stendahl. As for the unnamed speaker . . .

I know exactly who he is.

LYDECKER, DONALD M.

DOB: 8.5.1968

POB: Panama City, FL

MARITAL STATUS: Widower

KNOWN RELATIVES: (wife)(deceased)

CURRENT STATUS: Unknown

Served in Panama, Kuwait, Somalia
Promoted captain, assigned Delta Force
Legion of Merit, Purple Heart
Dishonorable Discharge 1995
ADAP 1996
Reinstated, assigned Project Manticore 2003.
Promoted to colonel, LTC Manticore 2004.
Supervised X-series training.

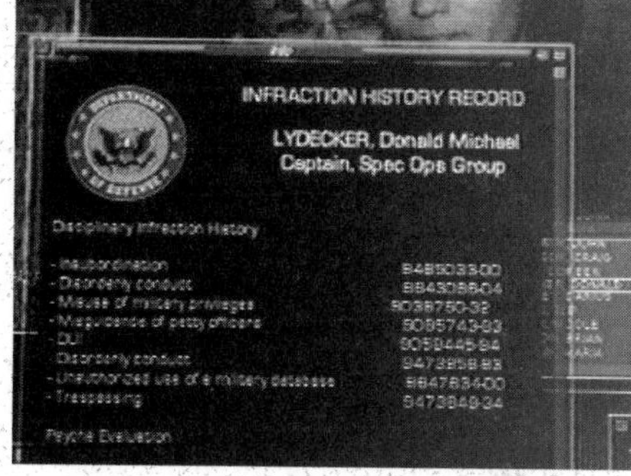

NOTES:

November 2019—May 22 takeover of genetics conference, Lydecker involvement in Jon Darius disappearance—death? See files May 22, Grand Coulee Massacre.
March 2020—X5 serial killer—see training photos, Manticore file, X5 493 notes.
May 2020—Manticore Assault
October 2020—Disappearance in "traffic accident"—see photos, conclave file, file Ames White.
December 2020—Hacked into his voice mail—various messages. Complete file available from Mac.

It wasn't any surprise to see Lydecker's name pop up in connection with Phoenix. He'd run Manticore for twenty years—trained every soldier who came out of there. "His kids," as he liked to call them. It seemed clear that one of those kids had killed the pope.

But a lot more than the pope's assassination was preying on my mind now. That had become part of a far bigger story—Phoenix. And probability that Manticore soldiers were being used to fulfill its ends.

I'd been hearing about those soldiers, and working with them, for years. Seth and Max, Zack and Tinga, Alec and Cece and Gem—from series X1 right on up through series X8. I considered myself as close as there was to an expert on Manticore, and what had gone on there.

But in the transcript Dazzler had gotten me, Lydecker talked about series X5R. In all the investigating I'd done, I'd never come across that reference before.

I wondered if anyone else had.

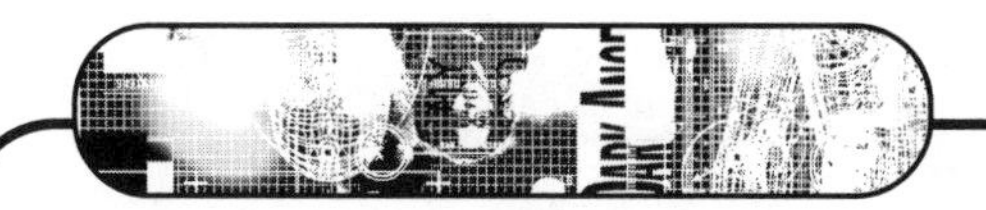

TO: iionly@pfpfree.net

FROM: seb2009@pfpfree.net

DATE: 2/17/21

RE: X5R

No connection anywhere that I could find.

R for a location—Reno?

R for revision?

R as abbreviation for a command group?

I'm just guessing, as I'm sure you can tell. I'll keep looking, though.

TO: iionly@pfpfree.net

FROM: asherman@pfpfree.net

DATE: 2/17/21

RE: X5R

No references on my end.

TO: mac123@pfpfree.net

FROM: iionly@pfpfree.net

DATE: 2/17/21

RE: Donald Lydecker

This is the guy whose voice-mail account we hacked into a few months back. See if you can dig up those files.

TO: iionly@pfpfree.net

FROM: dazzler@pfpfree.net

DATE: 2/17/21

RE: X5R

No further references, sorry.

I was stuck for a couple weeks there. I let the Phoenix investigation slide. A lot of other things were going on . . . Max getting shot, and almost kidnapped by the CDC. Ames White. Ray White. Ray Saunders. Getting out of my wheelchair for good, thanks to a blood transfusion from Joshua.

When I returned to Phoenix, I questioned as many of the transgenics I knew as possible, asking them about X5R. None of them knew a thing—not the X-series soldiers, not Mole, not any of the refugees holed up in Terminal City.

Dead end.

Then a breakthrough, from one of the computer files I had managed to salvage, with my notes on Dr. Adriana Vertes. She'd been part of Manticore from its earliest stages—finally left when it became too much for her, with what Lydecker was doing to his "kids."

But she'd been at Manticore after the '09 escape. From what she'd revealed afterward, the military brain trust had felt that maybe the X5s had been designed with too much independence. So the order had come down, and the X5s had been simplified. Their behavior altered.

Revised.

X5R.

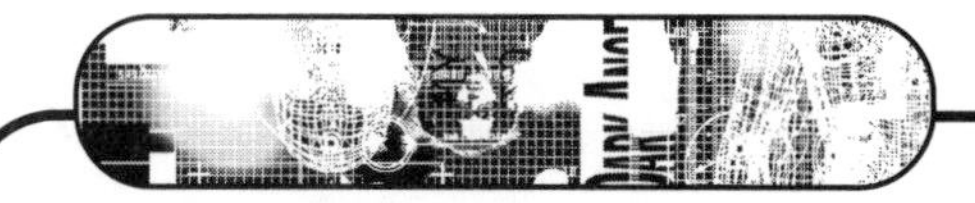

TO: iionly@pfpfree.net

FROM: thecolonel@pfpfree.net

DATE: 4/6/21

RE: Reassigned

I've been posted to special ops group operating off the McKinley, Pacific Fleet. This is my last week land-based, so I'll be out of touch for a while. Could be quite a while.

You were asking about Stendahl—you sure that's the right spelling? I knew a guy named Stendall—that's how he spelled it—back in Iraq. Met him during the last phase of Desert Thunder, when we had Saddam cornered in Baghdad. This never came out in the press, but we came within a day of losing him. The last of the Republican Guard armored units did a night sally out of Baghdad, circled around us, and cut our supply lines. It was nine in the morning, we were half a day out of the city and raring to go—and we were out of gas. Intel had it that the Chinese were going to send in one of their Stealth fighters to pick up Saddam that night.

It looked like after everything—two years of fighting, twenty thousand dead, half the country a radioactive wasteland—he was going to get away from us.

Then this Stendall shows up in base camp, thin, kind of nondescript guy, no insignias, just desert fatigues. Walks in on the CINC like he's dropping by to borrow a cup of sugar. Says his unit is just outside camp, they can do the trip to Baghdad in one day—on foot. All they need is our intel—where Saddam is hiding, where his troops are.

Fifty klicks in a day, CINC Lind says to him. That's not humanly possible.

You may be right, Stendall says, and then he smiles in a funny kind of way, and just stands there, waiting for the intel. Lind's about to tell him to go to hell, when Stendall gives him a number to call in Washington. Lind looks at the number, and then at Stendall, and then he dials. When he hangs up, he's looking at Stendall in a whole different way. Almost like he's scared of him.

Stendall walks off with our intelligence, and the CINC's blessing. And right around dinnertime, we get a call. Stendall, from downtown Baghdad. Damned if the son of a bitch didn't do it. Fifty klicks, in one day.

He had to be a spook of some kind—CIA, one of Ridge's "Runners," maybe—but I don't know for sure. Conversation about Mr. Stendall was not encouraged.

Sounds like the guy in your transcripts, though—walks softly, but carries a big stick. A mighty big stick.

Be careful.

TO: iionly@pfpfree.net

FROM: mac123@pfpfree.net

DATE: 4/7/21

RE: Lydecker's voice mail

The files you wanted are attached.

DECRYPTION: SECURE 8 DECRYPTION STAMP: 5/8/21 ORIGINAL TRANSCRIPT: 4/7/21 V = Voice-mail stamp, C = Caller

FILE CONTINUES

V: Friday, December 11, 10:20 a.m.

C: Hi Mr. Lydecker, this is Valerie from Consolidated Data Storage calling. I just wanted to remind you that your account is fifteen days past due, and to ask when we might expect to receive payment. Please call me back at 1-555-5434-0925. You can speak to any of the operators, and we're open until 8 p.m. tonight.

V: Friday, December 18, 4:20 p.m.

C: Hey, it's . . . me. Was hoping you could hook me up with another ex-Manticore doc. Last one left town in a hurry. Said your former employers were looking to kill him. Anyway, really like to hear from you.

V: Thursday, January 14, 10:30 a.m.

C: Deck, it's Jewel. Just wanted to give you a call, touch base. Believe it or not, I'm thinking about making the move finally—getting out of old AZ and heading for someplace cool. Moscow, maybe. Is that a crazy idea, or what? Give me a call, let me know what you think. I'll wait to hear from you.

V: Thursday, January 21, 8:15 a.m.

C: Hello, Mr. Lydecker this is Cathy from Consolidated Data Storage. We're trying to reach you regarding your account. If you could call me back at 1-555-5434-0925 anytime before 8 p.m. tonight to discuss this, that would be great. Thank you.

V: Wednesday, February 4, 8:00 a.m.

C: Hello, Mr. Lydecker this is Scott with Consolidated Data Storage. Your account is seriously past due, and we will be forced to cancel our services to you if we do not receive payment by the fifteenth of this month. The total now due is $110 exactly. If you need to speak with us regarding this account, or have any other questions, you can talk to any of our representatives at 1-555-5434-0925. Thank you. Good-bye.

FILE CONTINUES

DECRYPTION: SECURE 8 DECRYPTION STAMP: 5/8/21 ORIGINAL TRANSCRIPT: 2/26/21 V = Voice mail, C = Caller

C: Consolidated Data Storage, can I help you?

L: Yes, I hope so. I've been out of the country the past couple of months, and just picked up a few messages from you about my account?

C: Can I get your name, sir?

L: Ah—Donald Lydecker.

C: Yes, Mr. Lydecker. I have your account information in front of me. I see you're several months delinquent here.

L: Gosh, I'm sorry. Let me take care of that right now. Can I pay by EFT?

C: Of course. Let me set that up for you.

L: Great. Oh—one other thing. I accidentally erased some of the files you folks are keeping for me. Hard-drive problems. Can I ask you to send me the ones I need back?

C: That might very well be possible, sir. I'll switch you over to our tech department after we take care of your bill.

L: Great. Thank you so much.

C: Not at all, sir. Customer satisfaction is our number one priority.

L: Well. Consider me a satisfied consumer, then. I was afraid I'd never get to see some of those files again.

FILE CONTINUES

DO NOT CIRCULATE: CONFIDENTIAL AND PRIVILEGED

To: Platoon Leaders, X-Series
From: LTC Donald Lydecker
Date: 12.10.2010

Please be advised that as of this date, we have completed an internal review of the events that led to the escape of twelve X5 units last February. In addition to the recommendations outlined in Memorandum of Regulation Title 8B-2 regarding X-series subjects, the following actions are to be taken, effective immediately:

1) Officer training for X-series units is hereby discontinued.

2) Platoon leaders are further warned that all disciplinary problems within their units must be reported to neuropsychology division immediately.

3) Unauthorized assembly of X-series units in groups of three or larger is prohibited except in the presence of a platoon leader or special ops forces.

4) The following X5-series units are considered to be especially "at risk" for aberrant behavior and should be transferred to neuropsychology immediately for reindoctrination:

X5 001
X5 102
X5 206
X5 211
X5 345
X5 387
X5 418
X5 453
X5 472
X5 494
X5 600
X5 657
X5 735
X5 798

Lydecker

To: Platoon Leaders, X-Series
From: LTC Donald Lydecker
Date: 5.9.2010

Please be advised that as of this date, the following X5 units have successfully completed reindoctrination. Because of the length of time they have spent apart from the other platoons, these units will now continue their training under the command of SFC Parker.

X5 102
X5 206
X5 211
X5 345
X5 387
X5 418
X5 453
X5 472
X5 494
X5 600
X5 657
X5 735
X5 798

Internally, these units are now to bear the designation X5R to indicate successful completion of mandatory pyschological reconditioning.

cc: Martin Engel
James McGinnis
John Payson
Frank Sandoval
Davis Stendahl
Werner Stutzman
Adriana Vertes

TO: LTC Donald Lydecker
FROM: SFC Parker
DATE: 5.10.2017
RE: X5R Operational Status

The following units have completed training (courses in METT-T, OCOKA, and special ops) and are now certified for field deployment:

X5R 453
X5R 472
X5R 494
X5R 600
X5R 657
X5R 735
X5R 798

The following units failed to complete the necessary training:

X5R 102
X5R 345
X5R 387
X5R 418

X5R 206 and X5R 211 were damaged during training exercises, and subsequently destroyed.

DO NOT CIRCULATE: CONFIDENTIAL AND PRIVILEGED

TO: SFC Parker
FROM: Lydecker
RE: X5R
DATE: 5.14.2017

I am hereby ordering reclassification of the following units:

X5R-453. This unit has been requested by Division 12 for other deep-cover work and should be transported to their Fort Brevard facility asap.

X5R-494, X5R-798. Further disciplinary training of these units is required. They will be returned to platoon.

The remainder of the units are being reassigned to special ops Quantico, and should be prepped for immediate transport 5.15.2017 0800 hours.

TO: Stendahl
FROM: Lydecker
RE: X5R
DATE: 5.21.2017

Your team is on the way: platoon designation Arizona.

Dossiers follow. The names are ones they gave each other during training. I'm not in favor of allowing their continued usage, but it's your call.

Designation: 33223141 8472—"Devon"
Group: X5R
DOB: 6.7.2000
POB: Vivadyne Labs
HT: 6'1"
WT: 165
HAIR: Black
EYES: Brown
BLOOD: UD

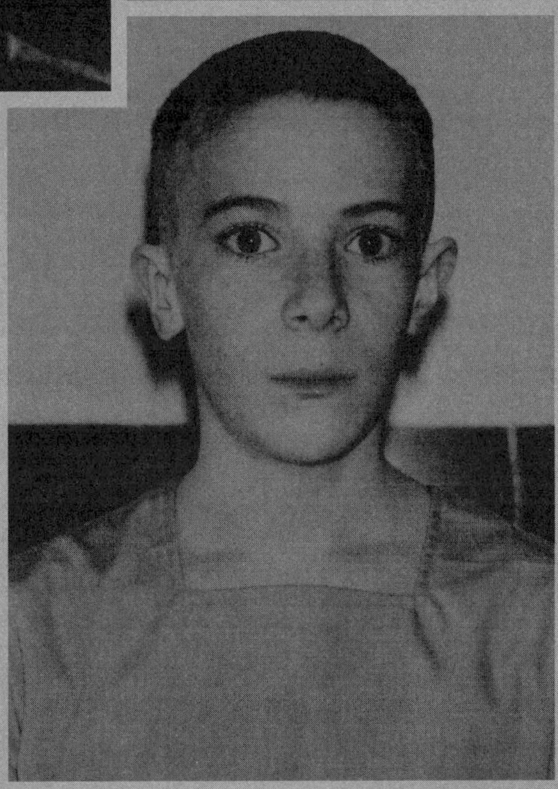

NOTES:

Enhanced survival capacity:
Unit optimized for extended missions
Estimated 10-day survival time in
absence of supplies
Weapons training:
P90 Submachine Gun
M-9 Pistol

Submitted, 5.1.2017
SFC Parker

Designation: 330417291600—"Lane"
Group: X5R
DOB: 2.6.1998
POB: Vivadyne Labs
HT: 5'10"
WT: 180
HAIR: Blond
EYES: Blue
BLOOD: UD

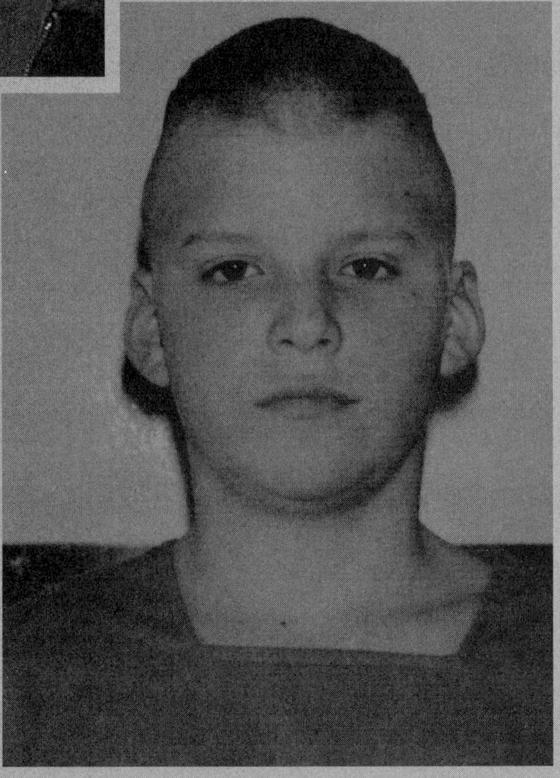

NOTES:

Increased muscle fiber density:
Unit optimized for hand-to-hand combat
Weapons training:
- P90 Submachine Gun
- M-9 Pistol
- Kalashnikov Assault Rifle
- Neumann U-87

Extraordinary weapons proficiency

Submitted, 5.1.2017
SFC Parker

Group: X5R
DOB: 4.24.2000
POB: Vivadyne Labs
HT: 5'7"
WT: 135
HAIR: Black
EYES: Black
BLOOD: UD

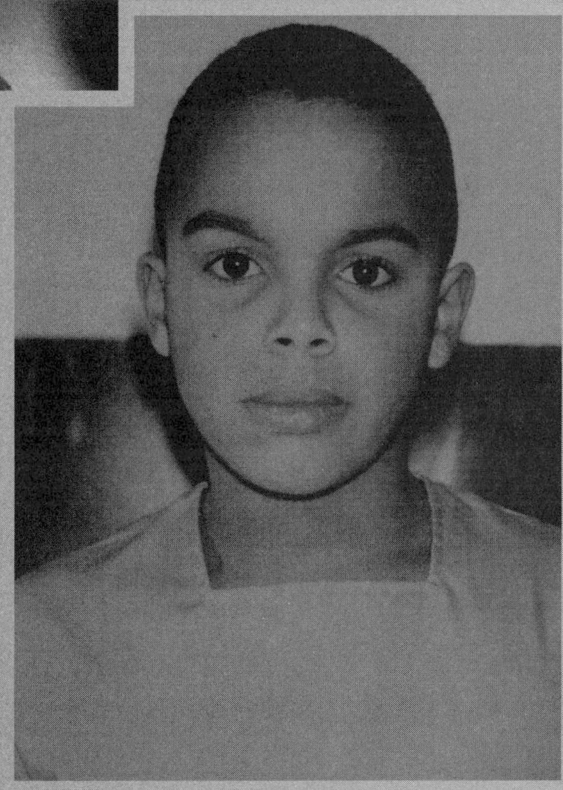

NOTES:

Heightened sensory capacity:
Unit optimized for night warfare
Weapons training:
P90 Submachine Gun
Colt M-4
Disciplined 11.15.2016—Infraction of rules regarding contact with command personnel,
unauthorized off-site travel
Disciplined 4.5.2017—Unauthorized contact with command personnel

Submitted, 5.1.2017
SFC Parker

Designation: 331280315735—"Keema"
Group: X5R
DOB: 7.1.1999
POB: Vivadyne Labs
HT: 5'6"
WT: 118
HAIR: Black
EYES: Black
BLOOD: UD

NOTES:

Heightened muscular flexibility:
Unit optimized for hand-to-hand combat
Weapons training:
    P90 Submachine Gun
    Colt M-4

Submitted, 5.1.2017
SFC Parker

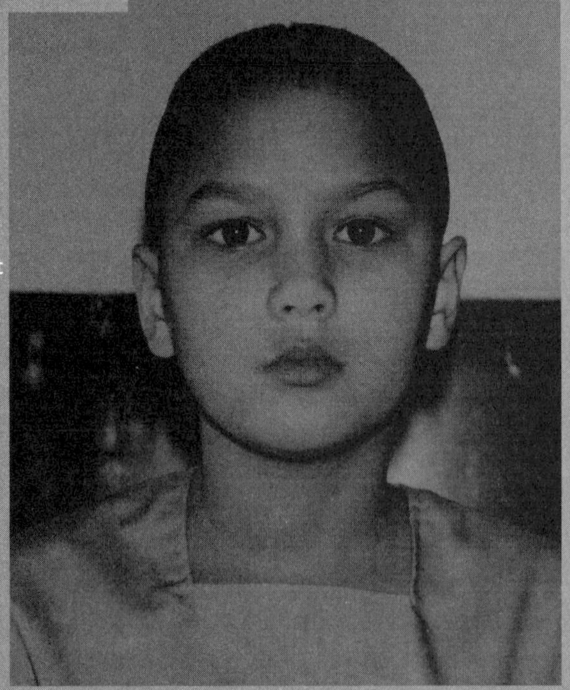

OFFICE OF THE DIRECTOR

DO NOT CIRCULAT
CONFIDENTIAL AN
PRIVILEGED

TO: Lydecker

FROM: Renfro

DATE: 5/1/2020

RE: Arizona

As discussed, we're implementing a policy shift with regard to this platoon. Please forward all relevant documentation to me, as well as a copy of the original Phoenix Project memorandum.

TO: Renfro

FROM: Lydecker

DATE: 5/4/2020

RE: Arizona

I understand that a new policy directive regarding the above platoon has already been issued, so my comments will have little bearing on the situation in the field. Nonetheless, I want to go on record as being completely opposed to the change in protocol.

Insertion of X5R units in deep-cover situations is tantamount to a recipe for disaster. By training and disposition, these units do not have the capability to function independently of a field officer. Once given an assignment, they may carry it out competently, but you know as well as I do that no operation goes exactly as planned. Inevitably, complications will arise, which they will be unable to deal with, and it is almost certain that exposure will result—with disastrous consequences for the unit and the program as a whole.

If I may be frank: if you were looking for a way to destroy Manticore, you couldn't do better than by implementing this policy.

Lydecker

DO NOT CIRCULATE:
CONFIDENTIAL AND
PRIVILEGED

OFFICE OF THE DIRECTOR

TO: Lydecker

FROM: Renfro

DATE: 5/4/2020

RE: Arizona

Thank you for your comments, Deck.

You know how much I appreciate the frank exchange of views. But I'm afraid we'll have to agree to disagree on this one: the units have already been given their new assignments, and plans are being drawn up for deep-cover insertion.

By the way, I wouldn't worry too much: they seem like smart kids. I'm sure they'll do just fine.

P.S.—
Thought you would be interested—we've chosen X5R 600 for the Rome assignment. The kid takes a nice picture, doesn't he?

The Secretary of State
of the United States of America
hereby requests all whom it may concern to permit the citizen/
national of the United States named herein to pass
without delay or hindrance and in case of need to
give all lawful aid and protection.

Brian Pollack

SIGNATURE OF BEARER

NOT VALID UNTIL SIGNED

UNITED STATES OF AMERICA

PASSPORT

Type
J

Code of Issuing/State
USA

Passport No.
9843092

Surname
POLLACK

Given Names
BRIAN MICHAEL

Nationality
UNITED STATES OF AMERICA

Date of Birth
12 SEP 01

Sex
M

Place of Birth
WYOMING, U.S.A.

Date of Issue
27 APR 18

Date of Expiration
26 APR 28

J<USAPOLLACK<<BRIAN<MICHAEL<<<<<<<<<<<<<<<<<<<<<
9843092ZEDA990389200CK<<<<<<<<<<<<<<<<<<<<<<<<<<

Renfro put X5R 600—or "Lane," if you prefer—on a C-141 to Guidonia AFB in Rome. He did his job there. He killed the pope.

Mystery solved. Case closed. Except . . .

The other three X5Rs. In her memo to Lydecker, Renfro said they'd been given their assignments. No way of knowing what those assignments were, or where they are today. Renfro is dead. Manticore is gone. Lydecker's missing, and Stendahl seems to have disappeared off the face of the earth.

Which leaves only the X5Rs themselves. Devon, Keema, and Jewel. Jewel, who left a message on Lydecker's answering machine several months back.

"I'm thinking about heading someplace cool—maybe Moscow . . . give me a call. Let me know what you think."

It sounds as if she's waiting for instructions. Waiting to find out if she should carry out some previously arranged assignment, or not.

It's a safe bet what that assignment is.

The new Russian president—Nikolai Kolankov—has been remarkably successful at rebuilding the Soviet military machine. Some say he's preparing to confront the coalition forces currently occupying Turkey. To those people, Kolankov represents the same kind of threat to Phoenix objectives Pope Leo did.

The kind of threat Manticore—and series X5R—were created to deal with.

Jewel's picture has already been sent out over the Informant Net, to sources in Russia. No word back yet on whether anyone's spotted her.

Keep track of that. Keep your eyes—and ears open—for the other two, as well. And try to find Stendahl—it's likely he's the key to the entire Phoenix operation.

Good luck.

THE GRAND COULEE MASSACRE

The Grand Coulee Massacre

Crossfile:

Maurice Beltran

Jon Darius

Yukio Tanaka

Jude Thatcher

THE GRAND COULEE MASSACRE

July 12 2017

Forty-five people Died Marching for Justice

Honor their memory

ANNIVERSARY MARCH ON THE GRAND COULEE DAM SUNDAY JULY 12 2021

Four years ago, several hundred Seattle residents marched on the Grand Coulee Dam to demand an end to the power outages plaguing their city. The Protectorate's National Guard Troops countered that peaceful protest with bullets. When the day was done, forty-five innocent demonstrators had been murdered.

Remember their lives

Remember their message

NO MORE BLACKOUTS!!!

NO MORE SCHEDULED OUTAGES

Citizens of Seattle

LET YOUR VOICE BE HEARD

Seattle City Light and Power Owns the Grand Coulee Dam
You, the residents of Seattle, own this dam
America's largest producer of hydroelectric power
80,000 kilowatts per day
Where is the power we pay for going?

Demand the Truth
Come March With Us
Buses Leaving from Various Sector Checkpoints

Contact
Sector 7 Council Delegate Lisa Herring
Sector 8 Council Delegate Andrew Seal
Sector 12 Council Delegate Arkady Hermann

The flyers are up all over town. Somebody wants to make sure no one ever forgets what happened at Grand Coulee five years ago.

But things aren't always what they seem.

July 12, 2017. People marched that day because they were sick and tired of living like third-world citizens, watching their tax dollars disappear down a seemingly bottomless black hole for nothing. Sick of seeing politicians like Beltran and Steckler living in mansions lit up like Christmas trees, while they didn't have enough power to keep their refrigerators running in the summer, or keep the heat on during winter.

They thought they knew who the bad guys were. Of course they were right—our last two mayors were both rotten to the core.

But some stories have more than one villain.

This is one of those.

It begins, in a way, with the day that changed everything.

June 9, 2009.

The Pulse.

The Pacific Free Press

Saturday, June 7, 2014 * 50 Cents

A FREE PRESS SPECIAL ISSUE:

POST-PULSE AMERICA:

Five years after the attack, how far have the mighty fallen?

Once upon a time, December 7, 1941, was our nation's "day of infamy"—our darkest hour, that moment from which it seemed we might never recover. A little more than twenty years later, on November 22, 1963, the American psyche was shattered yet again, when President John F. Kennedy was assassinated in Dallas. And thirteen years ago, on that awful morning that the twin towers fell, September 11, 2001, was added to that list of terrible, unforgettable days.

But now—and perhaps, forever—the day that will mark the nadir of the American story is June 9, 2009. On that date terrorists wrote R.I.P. to the Pax Americana and ushered in a nationwide depression that to this very day shows no signs of abating.

Sometime after midnight on that spring evening, a forty-kiloton bomb exploded over the Atlantic Ocean. The terrorists who set it off made it the dirtiest kind of bomb possible. They did their job well—the fallout killed close to a million people. That was bad enough. But what proved worse, in the long run, was the electromagnetic pulse the bomb generated. That EMP wiped clean every computer east of the Rockies—and in one nanosecond, America went from superpower to third-world country.

Over the next few years, food riots,

armed revolts, and in the New England states, the brief establishment of a rogue government, irrevocably changed the country's economic and political landscape.

Now, five years after the Pulse, though the United States government remains intact, the rule of law has disappeared. And in its place, the law of the jungle has returned—with a vengeance.

In this *Free Press* special issue, we will examine what has become of America since that June morning. Our

focus is on the West Coast and Seattle—but you'll also hear from Hunter Dylan in Washington, with a report on the new Supreme Court, and Jeanine Pearl in Hollywood on how Hong Kong has hijacked the movie industry—and the American myth-making machinery along with it.

Closer to home, Nathan Herrero takes a close look at Mayor Rene Beltran's bid for a fourth term, John Mercer takes a ride with the city's "last honest cop," and Logan Cale takes on the public education power structure.

We hope the issue informs and enlightens you. As always, feel free to write us with your comments.

And if you don't like what you read, do something about it.

That's the way democracy works.

The Editors

PLEASE DON'T LET ME BE MISUNDERSTOOD

The man who put Seattle under martial law wants your sympathy
And your vote, if you please

by Nathan Herrero

The first thing you notice when you enter the office is the flowers. After passing through half a dozen security checks, a seemingly endless maze of concrete corridors, and a sea of helmeted sector police, the colorful bouquets lined up along the credenza behind Mayor Beltran's long desk immediately capture your attention. Tulips. Lilacs. Roses. Dozens of roses.

"Courtesy of a friend," Beltran responds when I ask him where the flowers came from. It's a Sunday afternoon—the only time I could get an appointment to see Beltran—and the mayor looks like he's just come in off the golf course, sunglasses, polo shirt, khakis—very much a gentleman-at-ease. "Help yourself."

For a second, I think about taking one, for my daughter.

Then I take a closer look around the office, and see the other things Mayor Beltran's friends have given him.

Half a dozen bottles from Gates/Jackson Vineyards—pre-Pulse, no doubt.

Letters of appreciation on the wall from the governor, the secretary of defense, and the chairman of United Aerospace Technologies—along with a photocopy of a six-figure check made out to the Beltran Children's Welfare Society.

And I have to ask myself, what has the mayor been giving all these people in return?

In early 2008, Rene Beltran was a political neophyte, a businessman who appeared out of nowhere to ride a no-nonsense, "Make Seattle Work" platform to victory in the November mayoral race. And a little more than a year later Mayor Beltran, as even his most ardent critics will admit, was in the middle of fulfilling his campaign pledges when the Pulse struck. Which is when, according to those same critics, everything changed.

Beltran was the first mayor of a major American city to declare martial law. To help control a populace reeling in the face of sudden, catastrophic change, he rewrote Seattle's political map, dividing the city—largely along economic lines—into tightly defined sectors. He established a series of checkpoints, passes, and curfews that overnight split a diverse, thriving community into a group of suspicious, fearful enclaves.

Beltran promised the changes were temporary.

Five years later, though, the sector fences are still up. Martial law continues here in "the Military Protectorate of Seattle." And the city barely works at all.

Unless, of course, you have money to grease the wheels.

Then everything is for sale. The sector police. The city council. Housing permits. Sewer lines. Water. Electricity (courtesy of Seattle City Light and Power). You name it—if it's a service the city provides, there's a price tag next to it.

Beltran is a smooth operator. A handsome, confident man.

I'm frankly surprised he even agreed to see me, after some of the things the Press has printed about him.

Mayor Beltran: "From now on, everyone gets a seat at the table."

When we sit down for the interview, my first question is about the charges of corruption. He remains silent for a moment, and my first assumption is that he's holding his temper. But when he does speak, his words are calm, controlled.

"Look," Beltran says, "I know what a lot of people think about me. And I won't deny that I've cut some corners here and there, to do what I think is right."

Like defying half a dozen judges during his first term, when they ordered him to lift martial law?

Beltran nods. "Those were extraordinary times," he says. "The city was on the verge of complete chaos."

I concede him that point—though I feel compelled to point out to him that he similarly defied a judge's orders regarding freedom of the press issues on more than one occasion, as well. For example, from October 2010 to July 2011—arguably the period during which the most serious rioting occurred post-Pulse, as food supplies throughout the area ran low—Beltran shut down the *Pacific Free Press.*

There were reasons for that, Beltran says.

(see REASONS, p. 21)

Electricity for sale: that item intrigued me. Maybe it was because that was the summer the blackouts really hit in full force; the Mercy Hospital emergency room lost power during a particularly brutal heat wave, and three kids who'd been shot up in a gang fight died when they might otherwise have been saved by surgery. Big headlines.

Big story, I thought, and started investigating. How could life go on normally for some folks, and end in an instant for others? I had a couple of leads that looked promising for a while—but nothing panned out. No overt corruption rose to the surface, so I put that story on the back burner.

But the power outages kept right on, like clockwork. Before I knew it, a couple of years had gone by, and it was Halloween—time for my Uncle Jonas's big costume party. An annual "can't miss" event among Seattle society's crème de la crème.

I was a reluctant guest—so I made sure I didn't show up until just before eleven. I thought the action would be winding down.

I couldn't have been more wrong.

Please join

Jonas and Margot Cale

for their annual

HALLOWEEN GALA

Dress up for Drinks, Dancing, and all manner of Delights

9 p.m. October 31
The Eyrie
11 Rainier Path
Regrets Only 206-676-0902

LATE EDITION

Seattle Post

THE VOICE OF PUGET SOUND

25 Cents Plus tax

Tuesday, November 1, 2016

****

Kidnap Attempt Foiled

Terrorist Target Beltran in Botched Raid

by John Gergun
A Post Exclusive

November 1—Two armed terrorists were shot and killed late last night and two others captured during an armed raid on the Elliott Bay mansion of noted industrialist Jonas Cale. According to sector police, the terrorists—members of the radical May 22 environmentalist group—were attempting to kidnap Mayor Rene Beltran.

The incident occurred at approximately 11:00 p.m., according to police sources, when members of the May 22 group—led by founder Jon Darius—attempted to enter Cale's party by posing as invited guests. They were reportedly stopped by Cale's private security force, at which point gunfire was exchanged.

The assault put a premature end to Cale's annual Halloween costume party—a two-decade-old tradition among Seattle's elite. Among those in attendance were Mayor Beltran, Washington Governor Ann Godwin, former U.S. Senator Bob Bryan, and City Power Superintendent Maurice Beltran, the mayor's younger brother.

Why the mayor was targeted by the group remains unclear at this time; in the past, his policies have not been a source of controversy—at least among environmentalists. Cale, whose company is a leading supplier of weapons-specific military hardware to the U.S. and several foreign governments, has received considerable publicity for egregious pollution control violations on several occasions, and has more than once found himself and his company the object of outspoken demonstrations. He would seem to have been the more likely target, although police sources are sticking firmly to their conviction that Mayor Beltran was the May 22 group's intended kidnap victim.

Though police are not identifying the captured terrorists, they have stated publicly that Darius was not among them.

May 22 was founded in the wake of the Pulse and takes its name from the birthdate of Theodore Kaczyinski, the infamous Unabomber, whose manifesto remains the group's primary source of inspiration. Darius himself is a controversial figure who has engendered favorable publicity for his group in the past because of the respect he has accorded to all life, human and **(Please see page 22, page A4)**

Darius, Jon Christopher

DECEASED

DOB: 8.2.1986
POB: Cheyenne WY
MARITAL STATUS: Unknown
KNOWN RELATIVES: None
CURRENT STATUS: Leader of the terrorist group known as "May 22 Movement."

NOTES: A radical naturalist, Darius was founder of the neo-Luddite movement that drew its inspiration from infamous twentieth-century icon Theodore Kaczynski, aka The Unabomber. The group was invigorated by the effect of the Pulse and viewed it as a cause for celebration, not sadness. Recently, they have pursued a new line of terrorist attacks against the technology and modernism that have begun to reemerge in Seattle.

Darius was shot while resisting arrest, in a failed kidnapping attempt by his May 22 group.

He died November 21, 2019. R.I.P. is not the phrase that comes to mind for most people when you mention his name.

Burn in hell is more like it.

I understand where they're coming from. Perhaps better than most. The last time we met, he tried to kill me. He did kill several innocent hostages—and left a little boy orphaned.

But the man wasn't always like that.

JON CHRISTOPHER DARIUS

Reed/Sansevere College
International Politics
Bachelor of Arts

FALL SEMESTER 2002 SB 24309

PHIL 1001	INTRO PHIL	3	A	12
PHIL 203	EASTERN THOUGHT	3	A-	10.875
ENG 141	CREATIVE WRITING	3	B	9
RELI 101	INTRO HIST	3	C	6

12 12 37.875 3.18 12 3.18

SPRING SEMESTER 2003 SB 24309

ENG 146	INTRO LIT	3	A	12
PHIL 188	INTRO LOGIC	4	B	12
MATH 222	INTRO CALC	3	C	6
ENG 142	CREATIVE WRITING	3	B	9

13 13 36 2.769 25 73.875 2.955

FALL SEMESTER 2003 SB 24309

HIST 145	INTRO INTL REL	3	B	9
ENG 223	ADV CR WRTNG	3	B-	8
PHIL 233	EARLY 20TH-CENT PHIL	4	C	8
BIO 101	INTRO BIO	(4)	D	(INC)

14 10 25 2.5 35 98.875 2.825

LEAVE OF ABSENCE GRANTED 1/1/2004
REINSTATED 9/1/2006

FALL SEMESTER 2006 AK 154

C S 399	ADVANCED UNIX	4	D	4
POL 431	HIST TERROR	4	A	16
BIO 469	GENETICS	4	C	8
HIST 387	20TH-CENT AMER	3	C	9

15 15 37 2.47 50 135.875 2.72

SPRING SEMESTER 2007 AK 154

POL 998	SEMINAR GOVT	4	A-	14.7
C S 654	HISTORY MIL CODES	4	B	12
PHYS101	GEN COLL PHYS	4	D	4

12 12 30.7 2.56 62 166.575 2.69

DISCONTINUED STUDIES FALL 2007

END OF TRANSCRIPT

PILGRIM'S PROGRESS, OR ROAD TO RUIN?
THE INDUSTRIAL REVOLUTION RECONSIDERED

Jon Christopher Darius

Professor Sigal
Government Seminar
POL 998

A-

Jon—Excellent! Your historical research is exhaustive, your analysis of the last two hundred years incisive. I can't say I agree with all your conclusions (particularly regarding Kaczyinski), but there is no disputing the path you took to arrive at them.

The one flaw I see in the paper comes not on the historical level, but the psychological. There's a reason, for example, why everyone wants to be like Mike, or drink Coke, and it's not just because of corporate marketing strategy. It's because everyone wants that lifestyle. Important to realize the costs involved are not always best understood by a dispassionate analysis of the economic and/or political considerations—there is the human factor as well.

A minor quibble though; overall, this is an excellent piece of scholarship.

the last of the rain forests that the environmental movement gained broad enough support to force the U.S. and the first-world powers to reconsider their policy. Again, though, it was a case of too little, too late.

One individual who was committed to changing not just government policy, but the very idea of government itself was the Unabomber, Theodore Kaczyinski. In his infamous manifesto, Kaczyinski denounced the last few hundred years of human "progress"—what he called the "industrial-technological system"—as spiritually deadening and environmentally catastrophic. He believed the system had to be violently overthrown in order to prevent mankind from being reduced to mere cogs in a machine—in his opinion, sooner, rather than later.

It is clear from the examples on the preceding pages that the vast majority of people within not just industrialized society but the so-called Third World[1] shared many of Kaczyinski's concerns. However, because he chose to publicize his causes through the killing of innocent civilians, his actions had the effect of obscuring his message. Had he been able to find another way to bring those issues to the public's attention, he might have been remembered by history as a prophet, rather than a terrorist.

Nonetheless, a closer examination of his manifesto is still a valuable exercise: his analysis of the historical circumstances surrounding industrial technology's "triumph" over other societal mechanisms contains much illuminating, little-discussed information.

I begin with one of his most controversial contentions—that the industrial-technological system will eventually reduce man to a position of subservience to machine. Charts B and C (facing page) show, respectively, the percentage of workers in China's Hunan province employed in U.S.-owned factories, and the percentage of households possessing U.S.-sponsored cable television programming. The roughly parallel track of both graphs is not unexpected, but when a third factor, the incidence of obesity-related diseases reported

[1] I cover this gap from another perspective in the next section, "Secular and Religious Divides," in particular as it applies to the gap between the "decadent" West and the Islamic world.

In a lot of ways, Darius was like so many other bored rich kids of his generation. Looking for meaning in a world where nothing seemed to matter but the size of your bank account. You can see it in his studies—jumping all over the map, trying to decide what to major in, what to be. It's a feeling I knew all too well myself.

But like I said before . . .

The Pulse changed everything. For me, it brought things into focus. Showed me the world in black-and-white, good-versus-evil terms. It gave me something to fight for.

It did exactly the same thing for Jon Darius. I just hope that's where the similarity ends.

MAY 22

OUR CHARTER
OUR PRINCIPLES
OUR PURPOSE

We are May 22.

Our name has historical connotations that we do not deny; rather, we glorify our connection to the past. In the natural order of things, a man such as Ted Kaczyinski was bound to arise. Imperfect within himself, Kaczyinski was yet possessed of a perfect vision of the world as it is, and the world as it should be. A Moses for the modern era.

He predicted the Pulse, and events like it. And we, like Kaczyinski, see that occurrence not as a tragedy, but a call to arms against modern society.

We stand on his shoulders in proclaiming now our existence, and our principles.

We stand in opposition to technological society, and the system of control and subjugation it has spawned across our planet.

We stand with Nature, in all her wild, glorious freedom. Nature, that which is outside the system, and cannot be controlled by it. Nature, by which we mean all the creatures in this world interacting with one another and their environment in defiance of any artificial, imposed order, as intended by God and natural law.

We are May 22.

We wield the twin scythes of chaos and destruction—for from the gray ashes of technology's funeral pyre, Green will inevitably arise again.

So proclaimed, this 22nd Day of May 2008—

Jon Darius
Rachel Holman
Donald Mills
Sean Mills
Terrence Michaels
Petula Long
Dylan Fatt
Murray Page

Jeff Field
Anthony Cook
Paul Cook
Gem Castiglione
Leann Rafferty
Patrick Reilly
Flynn O'Connor

Alana Hart
Jason Smith
Donald Berg
Dave Martini
Paul Devers
Michael McCourt
D. A. Slater

Darius was smart. Those first few years, May 22 killed machines, not people. Panama, the Everglades, Del Muerto . . . he learned his lesson from Kaczyinski, I think. Don't alienate the people you're trying to inspire. Maybe in another

The Los Angeles Tribune

May 30, 2010

Terror Group Claims Responsibility for Tainted Beverly Hills Water Supply; Issues "Manifesto"

Christopher Livingston
ecial to the *Tribune*

everly Hills, California—A group self-styled anarchists calling nemselves the May 22 Movement as claimed responsibility for last week's attack on the city's water supply. The incident—in which a powerful food dye was somehow substituted for fluoride chemical packs at the city's Olympic Boulevard water filtration facility—caused tens of thousands of dollars' worth of damage to sensitive filtration equipment, and interrupted the flow of water to virtually all Beverly Hills residents.

Although no one was injured in the crime, police and federal authorities have classified this as a Class 1 terrorist incident and have announced their intent to prosecute the offenders under the James-Cheney statutes. If convicted, the persons responsible for the crime would receive a mandatory death sentence.

Those harsh punishments will potentially be meted out to members of the May 22 group. In an e-mail received yesterday evening by authorities and several area media outlets (including the *Los Angeles Tribune*), the group's leader, identifying himself as Jon Darius, accepted responsibility for the events in Beverly Hills and promised that further such attacks would follow. The e-mail stated:

"The water we drink, the food we eat, the very air we breathe is poisoned by the methods and by-products of the technology used to provide it. Beverly Hills, your water was tainted red to symbolize the blood of the Colorado River ecosystem, the blood of all the living creatures that died to provide water for your lawns, your pools, and the so-called green miracle that produced Los Angeles. We hereby proclaim that this miracle is a farce, and a perversion of the natural order of things." The statement was accompanied by a facscimile of the group's manifesto, and a call to arms, asking people to join May 22 in their struggle against the "industrial-technological system."

The group claims to be followers of Theodore Kaczyinski, the infamous "Unabomber" whose birthdate is May 22. Kaczyinski's own "Unabomber Manifesto," a rambling, semicoherent diatribe against modern society, called for the violent overthrow of the "industrial-technological" system.

According to Beverly Hills Police Chief A. Edward Foley, the group almost certainly had inside help in gaining access to (PLEASE SEE MAY 22, PAGE A8)

place, another time, he would have gotten his message through.

Maybe.

But not in post-Pulse America. Not after people began to realize that the good old days weren't coming back—ever. Nobody was interested in saving the whales, or the Rwandans. They wanted to eat. They wanted clothes for their kids. After a while, it made Darius angry.

It made May 22—and him—more violent. It explained his actions at my uncle's party.

But it didn't explain what Darius had wanted with Mayor Beltran.

That's what I needed to find out.

FROM THE DESK OF

Jonas Cale

Junior:

I don't know what you're looking for, but here's the information you wanted.

Uncle Jonas

NORTHWEST SECURITY
2156 IMPERIAL HIGHWAY
SEATTLE WA

November 12, 2016

Mr. Jonas Cale
11 Eyrie Way
Tacoma Washington

Dear Mr. Cale:

In accordance with your request of the fifth, we are providing you with a written transcript of the events that took place at your residence last month. As per our previous discussion, the physical recording of the event has been confiscated by federal authorities for use in their ongoing investigation.

The authorities further inform us that the person referred to in the transcript as "Intruder #2 (male)" has been positively identified via voice-print analysis as Jon Darius, founder of the outlawed May 22 Movement. None of the other intruders has been named.

Thank you for your continued use of Northwest Security: we greatly value your patronage and your confidence in our services.

Sincerely,

Walter Buchanan
President

NORTHWEST SECURITY
2156 IMPERIAL HIGHWAY
SEATTLE WA

This document is provided for the use of the Northwest Security client identified above. Any other usage is a violation of state and federal law.

Audio transcript 10-31-16
Listening Device: 12A (Front Entrance)
Time: 23:15 P.S.T.

Security 1: Roger that, perimeter check complete and secure. Next check is at 23:30 hours. Confirm? Roger. Out.

Security 2: Here come [unintelligible]. Check this out.

Security 1: Can I see your invitations please?

Intruder #1 (male): Hey, nice costume.

Security 1: Please halt right there, sir. Ma'am.

Intruder #2 (male): What's the problem?

Intruder #3 (female): Hey!

Security #1: We need to see your invitations, please. And some identification.

Intruder #3 (female): I get it. You're really security.

Security #1: That's right. Ma'am, please step back.

Intruder #2 (male): Hold on, hold on. It's in here somewhere.

Security #2: Sir, could you step back please—

Intruder #2 (male): Here it is.

[Gunfire is heard]

Intruder #1 (male): The son of a bitch shot me! Damn it. Damn it!

Intruder #2 (male): It's not bad.

Intruder #3 (female): Not as bad as that. Jesus Christ, look at all that blood.

Intruder #2 (male): Don't look. We have a job to do. Find Beltran, and bring him to me. I'm going to wait out here.

Intruder #3 (female): I'll be back.

[Unintelligible]

Intruder #1 (male): What the hell was that?

Intruder #2 (male): The walkie-talkie. Something's happening.

Intruder #1 (male): What is it?

Intruder #2 (male): Shit.

Intruder #1 (male): What are they saying?

Intruder #2 (male): They took out Peter and Sophie at the van. They know we're here.

Intruder #1 (male): Oh Christ. We need to pull back.

Intruder #2 (male): Not before we get Beltran, damn it.

[gunfire]

Intruder #1 (male): John, what are you doing? John, for chrissakes let's get out of here!

TO: citizenK@pfpfree.net

FROM: goodsinger@pfpfree.net

DATE: 11/29/16

RE: Darius's Accomplices

Not likely you'll get to talk to either of the May 22 folks captured last month—not in this lifetime, anyway. Beltran is prosecuting both under James-Cheney; Judge Newman is in session.

Don't even wait for the newspaper articles—they're going to be found guilty, and shot at sunup.

Sorry.

TO: iionly@pfpfree.net

FROM: goodsinger@pfpfree.net

DATE: 12/09/16

RE: Darius's Accomplices

Sorry it took so long to get this. Files on the two were sequestered until the execution. Now that they're dead . . . no problem finding out all about them.

The woman was Ray Holzbrinck, aka Rachel Holzbrinck, aka Rachel Holman. Darius's squeeze. Window dressing—a distraction for your uncle's guards. Nice house, as you can tell by the pictures, but according to my sources, nobody home.

The man, though—he's a whole different story.

Tommy Lewis, aka Tommy Long Cloud, aka Thomas Cloud, former deputy sheriff on the Colville Tribal Reservation, in the northeast corner of the state. Fired from his job over several accusations of brutality, trouble with his wife and kid, joined up with Darius a few years ago, was I.D.'ed as the trigger man in their attack on Synthedyne last year . . . a real piece of work.

Dear Mr. Call

I'm surprised you managed to find me, and don't know why you gone to all the trouble. I haven't had nothing to do with my boy Tommy for years—I don't know what made him hook up with your Darius.

I'll just say that Tommy wasn't a bad man, he just had a bad temper on him. Not a stupid man either—he's written some things here for our paper on the rez that needed to get said.

You asked me to call you, but I don't think I'm going to. I'll ask you not to bother me anymore.

Lois Cloud

FROM THE DESK OF

CARL DEDRICK

Editor, Confederated Colville Journal

Mr. Cale—

It was a pleasure talking to you this morning, and I'm happy to pass on with this letter a copy of that article we were talking about, the one Tommy wrote for the Journal.

To tell you the truth, I was surprised as all get-out when he sent it in. Tommy might've been a political man, but I didn't know him to have the kind of learning it took to write something like this. And the words he used...

Why, most of the time the article doesn't sound like him at all.

Anyway, if I do think of anything else that might be useful to you in trying to find this Darius fellow you're looking for, I'll let you know.

—C.D.

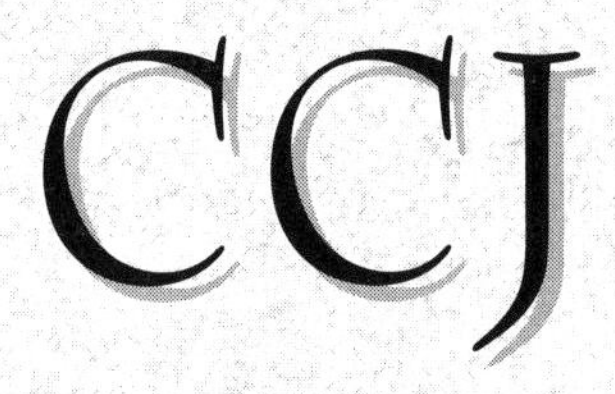

Confederated Colville Journal

The monthly newspaper of the Confederated Tribes of the Colville Indian Reservation—Nespelem, Washington

Volume XVI, Issue 2 February 2015

NO CAUSE FOR CELEBRATION

Viewpoint

by Thomas Cloud of the CCT

You can bet there will be some kind of celebration next year when the Grand Coulee Dam marks its seventy-fifth year of operation. Largest dam in the country, third most powerful hydroelectric plant in the world, it is an awesome structure, but forgive me if I do not join in the festivities. After you consider the facts of the situation, I don't think you will feel like celebrating, either.

Because for the Colville tribes, the dam was the last and greatest tragedy inflicted on us by the Federal Government. Its construction forced half of our population to relocate—without compensation. Our land was flooded, our hunting grounds destroyed, the graves of our ancestors desecrated. The great salmon and steelhead runs were obliterated, and these fish—the heart of our economy, once so plentiful—became an endangered species.

Now not even the eldest among us can remember a time before the dam, when what is now floodland was our breadbasket, the place where our people gathered along the riverbanks to collect berries and hunt game, to build our winter villages and sing our tribal songs. Where each year we gathered for a celebration of our own, the annual First Salmon ceremony, to pay tribute to the fish that sustained our civilization.

In short, the construction of the Grand Coulee Dam was a spiritually deadening and environmentally catastrophic project from which our tribe has never fully recovered.

We would be better off if the dam had never existed, if the great mass of concrete that prevents the Columbia River from resuming its natural course were suddenly to collapse.

We have been promised a fair share of the benefits from the dam by its new operators, Seattle City Light and Power, but like the Federal Government and the Bureau of Reclamation before them, they are long on words and short on deeds. What little power our reservation receives from the dam is often interrupted, and our farmers have yet to see their portion of water to irrigate their lands.

The Seattle city superintendent, Maurice Beltran, has promised to address these issues with us on several occasions, but he has yet to make an appearance at any of our councils. Worse yet, Beltran persists in the same tired rhetoric of the technocrats who wish us to look at the benefits the dam has provided for

(See Grand Coulee, Page 20)

Maybe Dedrick was right—maybe the article in the Journal didn't sound like Tommy Cloud. I had no way of knowing what Tommy Cloud sounded like. But after just a few paragraphs, I knew whom it did sound like.

Jon Darius—some of the phrases were the same ones he'd been using since college—spiritually deadening, environmentally catastrophic, to name just a couple.

And after reading that article, I suddenly had the feeling that Darius hadn't been after the mayor at all at my uncle's party.

He'd been after Beltran's brother—Maurice, the city power superintendent.

Still, I wondered why.

And more, I wondered if Maurice Beltran might have something to say about the attack.

Seattle City Light and Power
12 Republican Street Seattle Washington 98000

January 11, 2017

Mr. Logan Cale
The Pacific Free Press
21 Second Avenue South
Seattle Washington 98732-3332

Dear Mr. Cale:

Thank you very much for your recent letter. Unfortunately, I will not be able to grant your request for an interview at this time. The authorities have classified the events that took place at your uncle's party as terrorist activities, and thus, under the James-Cheney Act of 2008, I am not permitted to discuss them with media representatives.

Regarding the Colville Indian tribes, that situation is being closely examined, and I can promise you and your readers that this administration is firmly committed to seeing justice done after so many years. I'm afraid that access to those files, however, is strictly limited to workers who have been cleared by the Homeland Security Department.

Notwithstanding the above, I do wish you the best of luck with your article.

Sincerely,

Maurice Beltran
Superintendent

Seattle City Light and Power
12 Republican Street Seattle Washington 98000

Maurice Beltran
Superintendent

District Supervisors

Raphael Arnold
Johnson Black
Michael Bradley
Alison Graves
Timeo Jones
Jennifer Krc
Alan Lans Jr.
Laura Lenz
Janice Liberti
Karen Lobosco
Eileen Macy
Anne Mainberger
Craig Marchand
Gerald Nunnelly
Alison Peters
David Rutenberg
Dorothy Sanchez
Malloy Simkins
Yokio Tamamura
Vincenzo Volpe

Board of Governors

Marguerite Gosha
The Honorable Jon Hipps
Edgar Sonrisa
Leopold Steckler

January 21, 2017

Mr. Logan Cale
The Pacific Free Press
21 Second Avenue South
Seattle Washington 98732-3332

Dear Mr. Cale:

Your persistence is admirable.

My admiration, however, does not extend to the point where I can permit you to contact our employees surreptitiously. Just to make it clear to you and your paper, the information you seek is classified as vital to our national security, and thus falls under the James-Cheney Act of 2008. Any unauthorized use of this information will result in prosecution under the terms of that act, and I have been assured by our district Homeland Security personnel that the letter of the law will be strictly observed.

Sincerely,

Maurice Beltran
Superintendent

FROM THE DESK OF

CARL DEDRICK

Editor, Confederated Colville Journal

Mr. Cale—

Something that slipped my mind when we were talking. You said you were interested in any information about Tommy that I had—well, I'd forgotten he sent in his article via e-mail. The address he used was tommy22@greenworld.org—thought you might want that.

Stay in touch, and if you ever want to come visit our little newspaper and see how we do it up here, you just let me know.

—C.D.

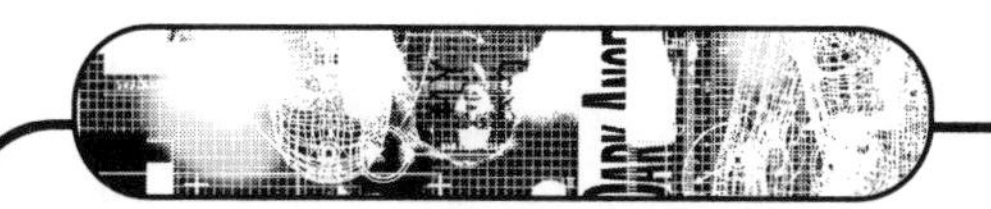

TO: iionly@pfpfree.net

FROM: seb2009@pfpfree.net

DATE: 2/3/17

RE: greenworld.org

That domain belongs to a company called—no surprise—Greenworld. Which, on the surface, looks like a legitimate corporation. According to corporate databases I scanned, they sell recycled paper goods. Their plant is outside Vancouver and their offices are in the city.

But . . .

Leave the virtual world for the real one, and you find a different story entirely. The address they give for their factory belongs to an abandoned schoolhouse. Their offices are in a half-finished building downtown.

Their only real asset is the domain name—greenworld.org. It resides on a server in Madrid, outside the reach of U.S. law.

I hacked onto it, and was able to access half a dozen e-mail accounts associated with the domain name before their security systems booted me off.

The list follows, though I think the one at the bottom is what you'll be interested in.

rholman@greenworld.org

mandrake@greenworld.org

tommy22@greenworld.org

Sloban@greenworld.org

Hermann@greenworld.org

jd22@greenworld.org

TO: seb2009@pfpfree.net

FROM: iionly@pfpfree.net

DATE: 2/3/17

RE: greenworld.org

Thanks. I think you're right about that last address . . . but I'm going to try them all.

TO: rholman@greenworld.org, mandrake@greenworld.org, tommy22@greenworld.org, Sloban@greenworld.org, Hermann@greenworld.org, jd22@greenworld.org

FROM: logan@pfpfree.net

DATE: 2/5/17

RE: Contact

My name is Logan Cale. I'm a reporter for the Pacific Free Press, and I'm looking to speak with May 22 and Jon Darius.

I have no agenda other than the truth.

TO: logan@pfpfree.net

FROM: jd22@greenworld.org

DATE: 2/5/17

RE: Contact

I know you. I know your paper.

Which is why I don't have you killed outright.

But we have no interest in talking to you.

My advice—and I'll offer it only once—is this:

Leave us alone.

TO: jd22@greenworld.org

FROM: logan@caleindustries.org

DATE: 2/6/17

RE: Contact

One question, and I'll do just that.

What do you want with Maurice Beltran?

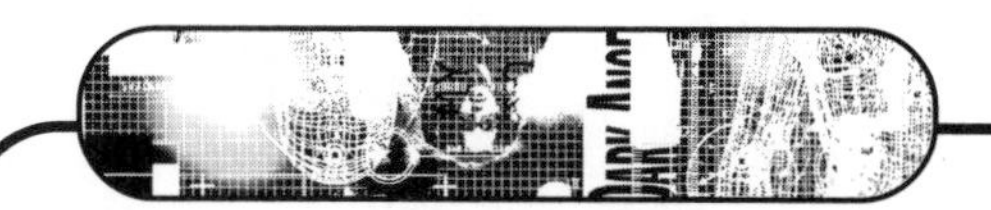

TO: jd22@greenworld.org

FROM: logan@caleindustries.org

DATE: 2/9/17

RE: Contact

Since you won't answer that question, Mr. Darius, let me take a crack at it.

Beltran is head of City Light and Power. You and May 22 have issues with him regarding the treatment of the Colville Indians.

I have issues with him regarding the blackouts that plague Seattle.

That, at least, should give us common ground to begin talking.

TO: jd22@greenworld.org

FROM: logan@caleindustries.org

DATE: 2/9/17

RE: Contact

Mr. Cale.

Perhaps we should meet after all.

The Pacific Free Press

Saturday, April 15, 2017 * 50 Cents

May 22 Reconsidered

An interview with Jon Darius, founder of the May 22 Movement

His name is high on Homeland Security's Most Wanted List—and right beneath his picture in the post office, you can find half a dozen other members of his May 22 Movement. He is responsible for half a dozen deaths, according to the authorities, and yet his movement has generated considerable sympathy, particularly among those most affected by the nationwide economic depression.

He is Jon Darius—and he chose the *Pacific Free Press* to publish his very first public interview.

Because Darius is a wanted man, we had to meet in secret. After several days of back-and-forth negotiations, we finally came to an agreement on terms for the interview, which included the requirement that we print what Darius had to say, unedited.

On March 8 of this year, I began my journey north to meet him. After I crossed the border into Canada, I drove to a ski resort near Vancouver. There, I was met by a young woman—in a ski mask, of course—and taken to another vehicle and blindfolded. After five hours of driving across some of the rockiest roads I've ever been on, we arrived at our destination. A simple log cabin, somewhere deep in the Canadian woods.

There, I finally sat down for a face-to-face talk with Darius. We found ourselves at odds almost instantly, when I opened our discussion by asking how his own parents felt about Darius referring to the Unabomber as a father figure. That contentious tone continued throughout our exchange...

So have you ever done an interview before?

No.

Why this one? Why now?

Because we speak to the same people—your paper and I. The ones who recognize this society for the sham it is.

The Press *recognizes that there are problems with this society—but we don't advocate tearing it down.*

You mistake my intent. This society will collapse of its own accord—my hope is to accelerate the process, and thereby minimize the damage done. From the ashes of the old society we will then reconstruct a new one—a just, equitable civilization, one that values human dignity as much as it does dollars.

How do you square that with the taking of human life?

Any deaths that have occurred as a result of our actions I profoundly regret. But the handful of people who have died in those instances is dwarfed by the numbers trampled by the progress of "civilization."

That's a pretty broad statement. Give me some specifics.

The Pulse.

War has been with us for centuries. And that was an act of war.

I'm not talking about how many died from the bomb. I'm talking about those who perished in the aftermath. You were there, Mr. Cale. You saw them—the people who starved to death, because food could no longer be trucked in on the scale necessary to feed Seattle's population. The people who lost everything—their homes, their jobs, the money in their retirement accounts—because of the EMP that went with the blast, the EMP that wiped clean the computers that kept track of those things.

Those people are still out there, Mr. Darius. How would your new society—your technology-free society—feed them?

We wouldn't, Mr. Cale. That's the harsh truth. Man needs to live in balance again with nature. That, at its heart, is what May 22 is about. Recognizing the need for limits on human development.

So you advocate population control?

Yes.

Forced population control?

If necessary.

That's harsh, Mr. Darius.

People need to recognize that there is a choice before us now—a choice about what kind of world we will live in. A world of concrete, and metal, and lives dependent on machines and technology, or a world in touch with the simple joys of living in harmony with nature.

So you're giving them a choice now? You won't pursue your objectives through violent means?

I didn't say that. Don't put words in my mouth.

I'm just trying to—

You're just trying to twist what I say, Mr. Cale. May 22 doesn't have the resources available to the technocratic state—the army, the Satellite News Network, the money, the machines. We are forced to use whatever methods may be necessary to get our message out.

You've used the press to plant your message before—albeit anonymously.

You're talking about the piece on the Grand Coulee Dam *(editor's note—see accompanying article from the Confederated Colville Journal).*

Yes.

Well. Now that we're speaking of this—I would like to make an announcement. We are planning a protest march on the Grand Coulee Dam for this July. I urge all your readers who share our views to join us.

That's something they may very well be interested in—given the fact that one of the people you're specifically targeting is Maurice Beltran. I don't suppose you'll be there, Mr. Darius?

In spirit. If I came in person—I'm afraid it would be the last anyone ever heard of me.

(See Darius p. 8)

Darius's invitation resonated with a lot of people.

Maybe it was simply the fact that they were tired of the blackouts, tired of the constant interruptions to their lives, tired of feeling impotent and unimportant. Whatever the reason, on the day of the march, they lined up by the hundreds.

I remember seeing them, all queued up for the buses, sector cops looking on, nightsticks in hand, wearing full riot gear on a day when the temperature hit eighty degrees by nine o'clock in the morning, and having a chill of foreboding run down my spine.

But nothing happened. In Seattle, at least.

When they got to Grand Coulee, though, everything went wrong.

LATE EDITION

Seattle Post

THE VOICE OF PUGET SOUND

23 Cents Plus tax

Tuesday, July 18, 2017

****

MASSACRE AT GRAND COULEE

Demonstration Ends in Violence 45 Protesters Killed as They Charge Guards

by Tony Lederman
Staff Writer

Grand Coulee—Yesterday's long-scheduled protest march on the Grand Coulee Dam ended in tragedy as national guard troops, confronted by a belligerent mob of protesters, were forced to fire their weapons in self-defense.

The violence marked a tragic end to a march that began peacefully and initially went off without a hitch. According to reporters on the scene, the approximately nine hundred protestors who arrived at Grand Coulee formed up into an orderly group without incident and proceeded down the main road, which guard troops had told organizers was the only route they would be permitted to use.

An isolated group of marchers sparked the violence when they abruptly attempted to breach a checkpoint that led directly to the dam powerhouse. Guard troops at the checkpoint fired warning shots into the air, and when those were ignored, attempted to use tear gas to disperse the demonstrators. What occurred from this point onward remains unclear, but at some point full-scale rioting broke out.

When it was over, forty-five protesters lay dead.

National guard spokespersons confirm that among them were two known members of the terrorist group May 22, apparently the two who triggered the initial conflict.

May 22's leader, Jon Darius, gave the initial impetus to yesterday's protest march in an interview conducted for the Pacific Free Press in April. Darius, already on Homeland Security's Most Wanted List, is now being actively sought on charges of inciting a riot and conspiracy to destroy government property.

(See Tragedy, p. 9)

I didn't understand.

According to the papers, it was May 22—prodded by Darius, no doubt—who had turned a peaceful protest march, by all indications a wildly successful protest march, a legitimate expression of civil disobedience—into a violent melee that cost forty-five people their lives.

Why?

I tried e-mailing Darius again, to get a response from him. Nothing. No reply to e-mails sent to any other member of the organization as well.

Weeks passed without another word from the group. May 22, it seemed, had disappeared off the face of the earth, leaving no tangible evidence of their presence.

But it occurred to me that there was the virtual avenue to explore as well.

TO: iionly@pfpfree.net

FROM: seb2009@pfpfree.net

DATE: 7/28/17

RE: greenworld.org

I find no trace of any activity on the server for the past several weeks. The group appears, as you said, to have gone to ground.

But your guess was right. They left files on the computer. Encrypted, but . . .

Not well enough to hide from me.

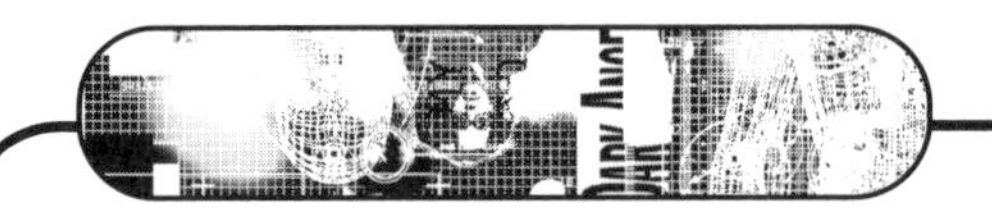

TO: rholman@greenworld.org

FROM: jd22@greenworld.org

DATE: May 21, 2015

RE: CLOUD

Don't sell Tommy too short. He's muscle, yes, but remember he's the one who let us know about the Colville tribes, and their dispute with Seattle Light and Power over the electricity. And that dispute is going to serve us well - it's a wedge, an entry point, a way for us to make a statement so emphatic no one will be able to ignore it.

I'll see you at the rendezvous next Monday, and we'll talk further.

TO: rholman@greenworld.org, mandrake@greenworld.org, tommy22@greenworld.org, Sloban@greenworld.org, Hermann@greenworld.org

FROM: jd22@greenworld.org

DATE: August 12, 2016

RE: <no subject was specified>

We have finalized plans for October 31.

The operation is to be code-named Greenpeace...for obvious reasons.

TO: jd22@greenworld.org

FROM: Herrmann@greenworld.org

DATE: October 8, 2016

RE: GREENPEACE

I must go on record again as opposing this. There are too many variables. The kidnap is not necessary - we have a cause to go there, though we need to wait till spring, or summer.

But having said my piece, I move on.

Starting Monday, I will be working in the Councilor's office. I don't want a record of this e-mail address at that location, so I will be able to check this only at nights.

Good luck.

TO: rholman@greenworld.org, jd22@greenworld.org, tommy22@greenworld.org, Sloban@greenworld.org, Hermann@greenworld.org

FROM: mandrake@greenworld.org

DATE: October 12, 2016

RE: GREENPEACE REVISION

Powerhouse 3, I've just learned, is closed for repairs. Therefore, we will now take Beltran directly to powerhouse 1. It is imperative that he remain alive long enough to sustain contact with law enforcement authorities to convince them not to mount an assault on us.

Access to the dam surface from powerhouse 1 is via security gantry, as illustrated in the accompanying diagram. Charge placement is approximate.

The hydraulic shadow, FYI, from this blast point increases to 5.7 miles.

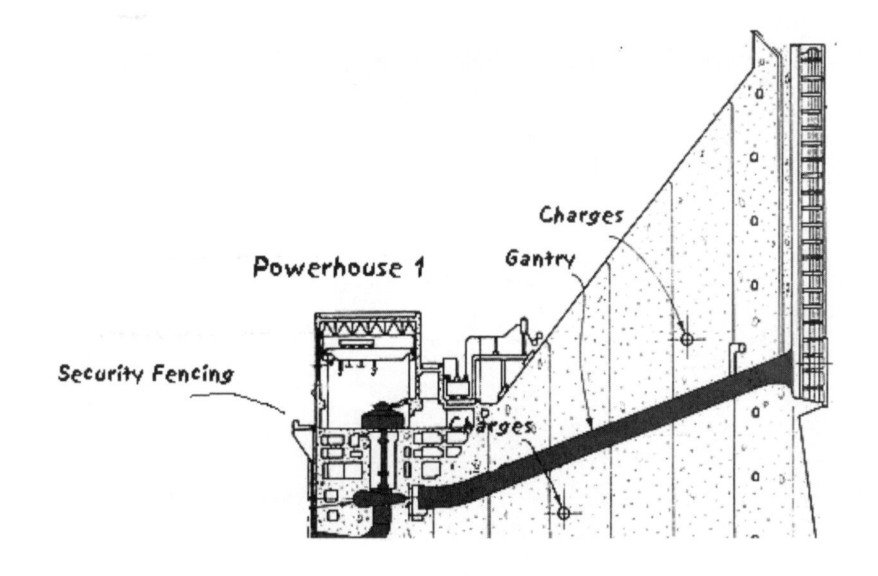

TO: Herrmann@greenworld.org

FROM: jd22@greenworld.org

DATE: January 29, 2017

RE: GREENPEACE

You were right, old friend. There were too many variables.

And having said my piece, I move on.

We try again. And again, and again, and again, if need be...until we get it right.

You have my permission to begin organizing the march.

Darius had lied to me. He'd used me, and the Free Press to publicize his march, when protest wasn't his goal at all. Protesting hadn't been his goal when he tried to kidnap Maurice Beltran from my uncle's party, either.

He'd been out to make a much bigger statement.

He'd been out to blow up the Grand Coulee Dam.

May 22nd's goal was to restore the natural order of things. They were going to destroy Grand Coulee to do that —never mind the thousands of people that would have died in the subsequent flood if they'd succeeded.

What does all this have to do with you?

Take a look at that flyer - the one announcing the anniversary protest march, at the very beginning of this section. Note the name at the bottom - Sector 12's councilman, Arkady Hermann. Hermann is new to the job — elected just last year, to replace Councilor Robert Dominguez.

Now look at the greenworld e-mails again. Note the ones from Herrmann - the Herrmann who worked in a councilor's office. The Herrmann who organized the first Grand Coulee March.

Is it the same man?

I can't be sure. The spelling is different. And I can't access records related to either man from here right now.

But one thing I know for certain.

Darius said May 22nd would try again.

It's up to you to find out if this march is their latest attempt.

Crossfile:

Manticore

Marcus Schuler

Donald Lydecker

Ames White

Davenport Genetics Institute

Davenport Genetics Institute

SPECIAL ISSUE: INSIDE "FREAK CITY"

THE NEW WORLD WEEKLY

AMERICA'S FAVORITE NEWSPAPER

May 9 2021 $10.00 plus taxes

BIKER BABE RULES MUTANT ROOST

HOT PIX!!!

WORLD EXCLUSIVE

CALL HER 452!
WHERE SHE WORKED AND LIVED! INTIMATE DETAILS!

PLUS!!

SPECIAL FEATURE—FACES OF THE FREAK NATION

5/8/21
Mole just handed me this.
Oh boy.

HERE SHE IS—

THE MOTORCYCLE MAMA WHO RUNS THE MUTANT ARMY

by Bill Leakey A *New World Weekly* Exclusive

Seattle Washington—Forget the flaming Xs around the fence—the hottest thing anywhere near Terminal City is the brown-haired beauty who gives the freaks their marching orders!

The barcode on the back of this gal's neck identifies her as "452"—but she prefers the name Max. And despite her size, this beauty packs a powerful punch. Powerful enough, according to exclusive *New World Weekly* sources, to tell the rest of her transgenic brood when to jump—and how high.

According to Seattle Police Detective Ramon Clemente, that's a good thing. Clemente gives "Max" the credit for resolving the May 4 hostage crisis at Jam Pony messenger service (see accompanying article) in as peaceful a manner as possible.

"We could have had a bloodbath on our hands that day," the detective told a group of reporters gathered outside police headquarters. "But thanks to 452—or Max, whatever you want to call her—every law enforcement official involved in that situation returned safely home to their families. I like our odds of keeping things under control—as long as she's in charge," Clemente added.

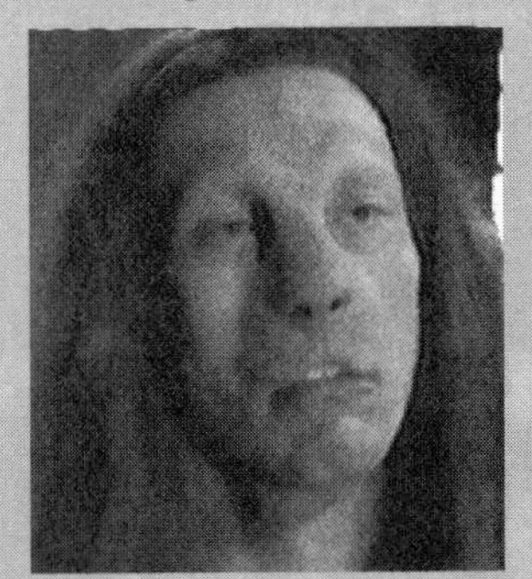

Dogman: Wanted For Murder

Detective Ramon Clemente

Others aren't so sure about 452's good intentions. They point to her close companion, known to *New World Weekly* readers as "Dogman," who is still wanted by police for his role in the April death of Seattle resident Annie Fisher. Fisher, a blind woman who had apparently been stalked by Dogman for several days prior to her disappearance, was found brutally murdered in the city sewer system after an extensive search.

Max herself has also been identified as a sus-

NSA Agent Ames White

pect in a series of robberies around town, though police point out that the ones accusing her of these crimes—including reputed drug dealer Reggie "Run-run" Cameron and his bodyguard Mack "The Hammer" Bean—hardly have immaculate reputations.

In all the controversy swirling around her, one fact remains clear. While "Max" may have the looks of a high-fashion model, readers should not forget that she is a test-tube creation—an experimental animal designed to fight to the death. NSA Agent Ames White—whom the *New World Weekly* praised in last week's issue for his recent testimony before Congress—warns us all not to let 452's appearance distract us.

"She is a trained assassin—killing is in her blood. Letting your guard down around 452 could be the last mistake you ever make."

The 411 on 452...

by the staff of the *New World Weekly*

While most of the transgenics inside Terminal City are newcomers to Seattle, their leader—the mutant known as Max—has apparently called our fair city home for quite some time. With that in mind, we here at the *Weekly* feel it only fair to give her the 411 treatment. So here's the facts—and a few well-informed guesses—about the mighty Max:

Height: 5'2"
Weight: 105 pounds
Dress Size: A perfect 4
Age: Only her lab tech knows for sure
Hair Color: Brown
Eyes: Brown
Favorite Color: Black
Favorite Movie: *X-Men*

Favorite Book: *Brave New World*
Turn-ons: Furry-faced freaks, Harley-Davidson bikes
Pet Peeves: Sector cops and federal agents

Think we're off the money? Know something about 452 that we missed? Don't just sit there! Write and tell us, c/o

The Editors
New World Weekly
1 Sasquatch Circle
Tacoma, WA 98138-0043

MORE THAN PISSED OFF . . . BEYOND ANGRY . . . HE'S . . . RANDY RAGE!

FREAKS GO HOME—AND GIVE US OUR MONEY BACK!

What's got me seeing red today, you ask? Well, like always folks, Randy is glad to tell you.

I'm angrier than an army of ants at a vegetarian picnic about these mutant weirdos I've been seeing on the old boob tube. They've taken over a big chunk of the Emerald City (that's Seattle, for you pasty-faced northeasterners) without so much as a by-your-leave to Mayor Steckler. Hey, I'm all for housing the homeless, but what are these sideshow attractions going to do for us in return? Suck on the old public teat? Randy don't go for that—though I gotta say what would work for me is number 452 barefoot and pregnant around the old RV. Yowza!

But back on topic, gentle readers, get this—apparently the Feds are the ones responsible for creating Maxie and her furry little buddies in the first place. When I look at what those scientist wackos did with your hard-earned government dollars, it makes me madder than a fox in an empty henhouse! Just have a gander at these creations, and see if you can tell me what in Sam Hill the eggheads were thinking when they cooked up these babies in their test tubes!

FACES OF THE FREAK NATION

Repent, for the End is Nigh!

Reverend Huey P. Hale

by Nathan Danielson

Get your Xmas shopping in now folks, because according to the Righteous Reverend Huey H. Hale, humanity only has one or two holiday seasons left here on planet Earth!

"I have received a message from the Lord," Hale declared. "In a vision, He told me a messenger from beyond the stars will bring forth a rain of death on our world—in the very near future."

Hale, who is a visiting fellow of interplanetary studies at Kidman Community College in San Francisco, went on to say that humanity is being punished for tampering with the Lord's ultimate creation—man—through the heretical use of science. Beings such as the transgenics holed up in Terminal City are "an abomination in the sight of God," according to Hale.

"They, and all those who stand with them, will be incinerated in a cleansing rain of hellfire from the stars above," the reverend told the *Weekly*. This rain of hellfire, Hale went on to say, will be similar to the one that sank Atlantis, and caused the great flood in biblical times.

This theory of periodic planetary extinctions, surprisingly enough, is one to which many scientists also subscribe—though they blame astronomical phenomena such as supernova and asteroids, rather than hellfire, for the massive die-offs of species. Many scientists even suspect that it was one such extraterrestrial visitor—an asteroid, or perhaps a passing comet—that caused the extinction of the dinosaurs sixty-five million years ago.

10,000-Year-Old Breeding Cult Creating Master Race Right Underneath Our Noses!

by Calvin Theodore
Special to the *New World Weekly*

The transgenics now flooding the streets of Seattle aren't the only threat to public safety—or even the most urgent one! That's according to Puget State College Professor B. Richard Boot, who says we should be much more worried about another group of people operating in the dark fringes of our society.

"I have recently uncovered shocking evidence," says Dr. Boot, "of a secret organization—one whose goal seems to be nothing less than the total annihilation of the human race!"

The group—a conclave whose members, Boot informs the *Weekly,* include some of our most prominent business and government leaders—descends in an unbroken line from the rulers of ancient Atlantis. Over the millennia since that fabled isle's destruction, they have apparently been hard at work perfecting their master race—and a plan to "empty the planet of those currently abusing her resources," in Dr. Boot's words.

That's you and me, folks.

Working with a group of "committed citizens," Boot has put together a wealth of evidence documenting the group's existence and tracing their actions down through the centuries.

"We have incontrovertible proof that they stood at the side of the great Egyptian pharaohs and had the ear of Augustus Caesar. We find pictographic evidence of their cult in the temples at Angkor Wat, on the caves in the Anasazi's secret dwellings," Boot told this reporter.

Moreover, says the professor, there are grave sites scattered across the globe that hold evidence of the conclave's breeding experiments—both successes and failures.

Boot promised to release this proof to the general public in short order—"once a few more pieces of critical information are in my hands."

Readers of the *Weekly* can rest assured that they will be the very first to hear details of this mysterious conclave, and their plans for worldwide planetary domination.

I used to wonder why people actually paid money for that rag. They must realize it's a joke—the articles, the pictures, the so-called sources, all of it. It would be too depressing if the public actually believed those things.

On the other hand . . .

Sometimes, they do get it right. The breeding cult story—that's White and his people, for sure. Sketchy wrote that article a while back. He told me the editors have been pressing him for weeks to find a new angle on the story. "Something fresh," they said. "Hot. Sexy."

What wouldn't they give to see these.

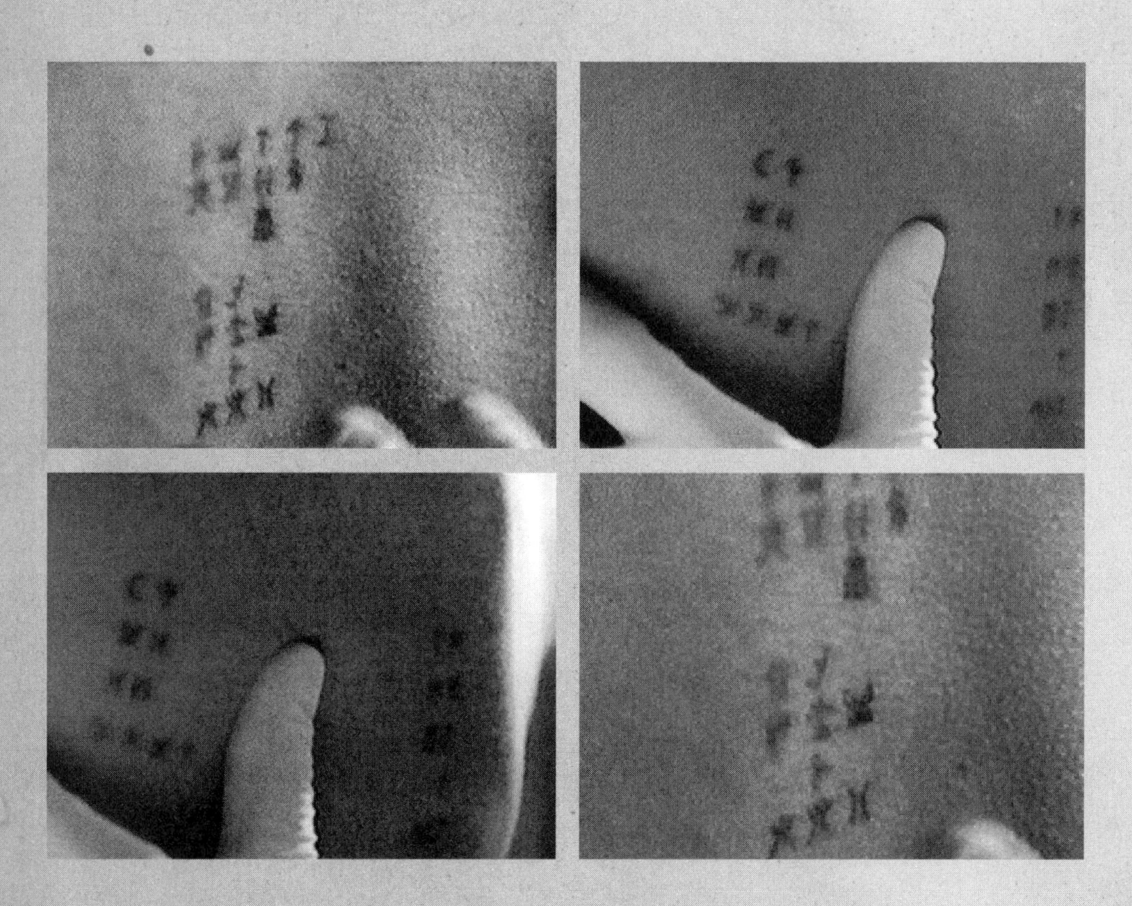

The body belongs to Max.

The letters are Minoan—a script called Linear A, that dates back to somewhere around 2000 B.C. They started appearing on her body a couple of weeks ago—it turns out they're part of her genetic makeup, like the barcode on her neck. Programmed into her, apparently, by a guy called Sandeman.

According to Joshua—or as the Weekly likes to call him, Dogman—Sandeman was the guy who actually started Manticore, and ran it until the military took over. For the longest time, Joshua called Sandeman "father." The symbols popping out all over Max's body are a message from him.

The symbols have multiple meanings, so they're hard to translate, exactly, but the gist of what's there is pretty clear. The message is something like this:

"When the shroud of death covers the face of the earth, the one whose power is hidden will deliver the helpless."

It sounds like something you find inside a fortune cookie. I've been looking for Sandeman to find out exactly what he meant—what the shroud of death is, and when it's coming.

Thing is, Sandeman's a hard guy to track down. I put the word out on the Informant Net—tried all the university records, medical records, passports, birth certificates, death certificates, etc., etc. Came up with absolutely nothing on the Sandeman.

And then right here in Terminal City, we found this.

SENT VIA FACSCIMILE TRANSMISSION 15169038732 110207

ADVANCED RECOMBINANT GENETICS

Suite 44-12 * Terminal City * Seattle WA 99830-8932

Marcus—

This will be the last you hear from me. For a long time—perhaps forever.

Don't expect to hear from the familiars you sent after me, either, old friend. Violence may pain me—but I am fully capable of it when necessary. Don't forget that.

I suppose it's my fault, for attempting a rapprochement. For thinking I could dissuade you and the others from the course of action you seem bent on pursuing. Technology has changed the world, and what human beings are capable of. You seem to have forgotten that at bottom, that is what we are—human beings. Not even ten thousand years of selective breeding can change that.

I do not bow to the wisdom anymore, Marcus. I do not bow to you. And I will never forget what you did to my sons, and to Natasha.

Sandeman

The letter was crumpled up in the back of an empty file cabinet—in an abandoned lab right here in Terminal City. A lab that belonged to ARG—Advanced Recombinant Genetics. Sandeman's lab—the place he came after Manticore. From the date on the fax, it seems as if he left ARG right about the time he left his house, heading for parts unknown.

Seems like he left on bad terms with this Marcus—who sounds like part of White's cult as well. But that letter was the only thing we found.

Not much to go on, I'll admit. But it was a starting point.

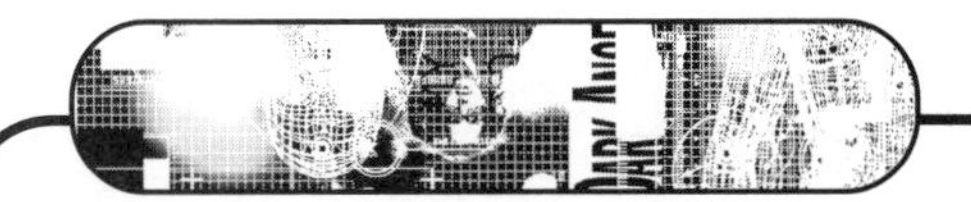

TO: iionly@pfpfree.net

FROM: seb2009@pfpfree.net

DATE: 4/28/21

RE: <no subject was specified>

Tried to run a D&B on Advanced Recombinant Genetics—no such company in the records, at least not anymore. Sorry. I've got queries out everywhere, but if they went out of business fifteen years ago . . . that's ancient history, in the biotech field.

TO: iionly@pfpfree.net

FROM: gatekeeper@pfpfree.net

DATE: 4/28/21

RE: <no subject was specified>

Nothing. Sorry.

TO: iionly@pfpfree.net

FROM: mac123@pfpfree.net

DATE: 4/28/21

RE: <no subject was specified>

Got a bunch of pre-Pulse phone databases here. No hits on the fax number on the letter, but the numbers on either side of it—5169038731 and 8733—come back to offices at the Davenport Genetics Institute.

TO: iionly@pfpfree.net

FROM: seb2009@pfpfree.net

DATE: 4/29/21

RE: Davenport Genetics Institute

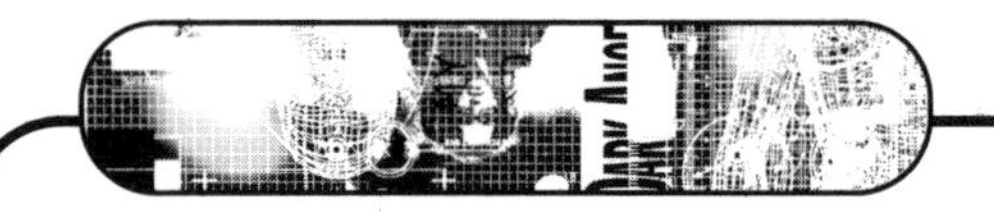

Davenport was the place to be back in the 1990s—they helped set a lot of the initial government policy on the human genome project. For a while there all the big names passed through—Watson, Holliday, Carlson—you'd be hard-pressed to find a geneticist who didn't put in some time there.

They shut down right after the Pulse, I think. Avoided headlines like the plague even when they were in business, which is probably why most people never heard of them. Only time they ever made the papers was when they were involved in some big scandal, right around the turn of the century. My memory's a little fuzzy on the details.

TO: iionly@pfpfree.net

FROM: asherman@pfpfree.net

DATE: 4/29/21

RE: Davenport Scandal

Fuzziness is to be avoided.

Details attached.

NEW YORK POST EXPRESS

THURSDAY, AUGUST 8, 1996

LI Research Facility at Center of Kidnapping Charges

as held.

by Brian Payton
Exclusive to the *Post Express*

Brooklyn—Police officials confirm that the prestigious Davenport Genetics Institute is under investigation for kidnapping and related sexual assault charges, based on allegations made by a young woman currently in protective custody.

According to sources, the young woman—twenty-year-old Josephine Morales of Elizabeth, New Jersey—was brought to the forty-fifth precinct at approximately 8:00 a.m. yesterday. The man who'd found her said Morales had been walking along the shoulder of the North Shore Parkway, barefoot and dressed solely in a white hospital gown. She told him she had been kidnapped by "the institute" and that doctors there had stolen her baby.

Based on her description and subsequent photo identification of the facility, detectives confirmed the institute in question as Davenport Genetics, located in North Lynbrook, New York. Contacted by this newspaper, an institute spokesman confirmed that Morales had been a patient at the institute, but denied all her charges. The spokesman also confirmed that the institute is cooperating with authorities in their investigation.

Davenport Genetics Institute was established in the early 1930s as a center for the study of eugenics, and over the years transformed itself into one of the premier research institutions in the country. The institute, in addition to its laboratory facilities, maintains an on-premises hospital, which is where Morales alleges she w

DECRYPTION: SECURE 8 DECRYPTION STAMP: 5/8/21 ORIGINAL TRANSCRIPT: 5/01/21 L = Cale, Logan, P = Payton, Brian

FILE BEGINS

P: Hello?

L: Yes, I'm looking for Brian Payton.

P: You got him.

L: The Brian Payton who was a reporter for Post Express, back in the 1990s?

P: That's me.

L: Good. Mr. Payton, my name is Logan Cale. I'm a journalist myself, out in Seattle, and I'm working on a piece—

P: Seattle? You're calling me from Seattle?

L: Yes.

P: Jee-sus. Haven't talked to anybody from the West Coast in years. I used to get out there all the time, back in the day. What's it like out there now? Martial law still, right?

L: Yes, sir. Still the protectorate.

P: And a curfew? You still have a curfew?

L: That's right.

P: Christ. Never thought I'd see the day. A curfew in the United States of America. Guess you live long enough, you see everything.

L: Yes, sir.

P: But I assume you didn't call me up to bitch about your lot in life. What can I do for you?

L: Your name came up in regard to a piece I'm working on, regarding the Davenport Genetics Institute? Do you remember—

P: Are you going after them? You better be armed for bear, son. Those bastards play dirty.

L: Sir?

P: The Morales girl. What they did to her. What they did to me, and the story.

L: Back up a second, if you would. All I know about Davenport is the kidnapping—the scandal that came with that.

P: Scandal? That wasn't a scandal. That was a whitewash.

L: It closed the place down though—didn't it?

P: They closed down when they were damn good and ready. A few years after the kidnapping, yes—but none of them ever went to jail.

L: So the charges against them were true?

P: They were true, and they weren't the half of it. They got away with murder.

L: What do you mean?

P: Just what I said. And the Morales girl wasn't the only one. She was the first one that got away, though. The others—they killed them all. The girls, and their babies.

L: I see.

P: Mr. Cale? You all right?

L: Yes. This conversation is connecting a lot of dots for me, Mr. Payton. Would you mind if I taped our talk, so I can refer to it later?

P: That's no problem. Got nothing to lose, now.

L: Good. Then let me ask you a few specific questions. Did you ever hear of anyone named Marcus in connection with the institute?

P: No.

L: He may have been one of the people running the institute.

P: No. No Marcus. I remember Dr. Hill, and Dr. Crater, and Sandeman, and—

L: Sandeman was at the Davenport Institute?

P: That's right. Listen, let me save you some time here. Send you my notes on the story.

L: Your notes.

P: Yeah, I have a whole file folder full of stuff. It includes my interview with Morales. The entire transcript. You want it?

L: Absolutely I want it.

FILE CONTINUES

TO: FILE

FROM: PAYTON

DATE: 8/10/96

RE: MORALES INTERVIEW, SESSION 2

Payton: So let's just pick up where we left off, all right Miss Morales?

Morales: All right. You could call me Josie, you know.

Payton: All right. You want a glass of water, Josie?

Morales: Water would be nice.

Payton: Hold on.

Payton: Okay. So yesterday, you were talking about meeting this guy–

Morales: John. I never even knew his last name. I met him at El Rubio's.

Payton: You waited on his table?

Morales: That's right.

Payton: Go on.

Morales: Well, you know. I mean, we were hitting it off, you know? And he was with some friends, and they left, and he hung out at the bar until I finished.

Payton: And then?

Morales: We hung out, you know. Went dancing, and drinking, only now that I think about it, I was doing all the drinking, and he was just asking me questions, all these weird questions, like where was I from, how old was I. What about my parents, my grandparents, were they still alive, were they healthy, where were they from–weird stuff.

Payton: All right.

Morales: I mean, now it doesn't seem so weird, you know?

Payton: No. Those questions make perfect sense. He was trying to find out your family's genetic history.

Morales: That's right. I thought we were like—hooking up, you know? And he's thinking about me like a lab rat.

Payton: I know.

Morales: Bastard.

Payton: Why don't you go on?

Morales: Well, so I don't hear from him the next few days. Then he shows up at the restaurant again—only this time he's with an older guy. And he's all weird and formal like.

Payton: This is John you're talking about? Who was formal?

Morales: Yeah. I think it was because of the guy with him.

Payton: Who was the older guy?

Morales: Sandman. The guy I told you about yesterday.

Payton: Sandeman.

Morales: Whatever.

Payton: And what did they say?

Morales: They told me about the institute. They asked me to come down and see it.

Payton: Did they offer you money then?

Morales: Yes.

Payton: How much?

Morales: A thousand dollars for the day. Just to come talk with them. Only they said I'd have to sign these forms—

Payton: The nondisclosure forms.

Morales: Yeah. Those. So I said sure. I mean, a thousand dollars. I was like—whatever. Stupid, right?

Payton: You couldn't have known.

Morales: So that's it. The next day they sent a car for me, and I went down. Signed the forms, and they made me the offer. Fifty thousand if I participate in the program.

Payton: If you get pregnant.

Morales: No, see, that was the trick. Fifty thousand if I have a baby for them. It wasn't just the getting pregnant part. Should have had a lawyer look the damn thing over.

Payton: Yeah. I hear that. Anytime anyone asks you to sign anything, have a lawyer look it over.

Morales: Yeah.

Payton: And you said yes?

Morales: Of course I said yes, what are you fucking crazy? Fifty thousand bucks–that's more money than I'm ever gonna see in my life. Only thing was, I miscarried two months in. So I go to see the bastards, and they say no baby, no money. But I'm free to try again.

Payton: Jesus Christ.

Morales: Exactly what I said.

Payton: Back up a second. What did they say when they made you the offer–why did they want you to do it?

Morales: Well, I don't remember a lot of that, to be honest. After they mentioned the fifty thou, I couldn't think about anything else, you know?

Payton: Do you remember any of it? Think back. You're sitting in their office–whose office were you in? Sandeman's?

Morales: That's right. He was there, and John was there, and some creepy old man came in about halfway through and patted me on the head. Uggh. Gave me the creeps–that was the only time I had second thoughts about the whole thing, you know? When that old man touched me.

Payton: Do you remember his name?

Morales: Ummm. No, sorry.

Payton: And nothing at all about what they said?

Morales: Something about how I was an excellent physical specimen–I remember that.

Payton: Well. You're a good-looking young woman.

Morales: You should have seen me before, mister. I feel like I've aged about twenty years in the last two.

Payton: It doesn't show.

Morales: Thank you.

Payton: You're welcome. So–you told them you'd get pregnant, and you signed the papers, and then . . .

Morales: And then, I got pregnant.

Payton: How?

Morales: What do you mean how?

Payton: Artificial insemination, or–

Morales: Hell no. Nothing artificial about it. John and I went into one of the hospital rooms there and did it–I mean, it was a few days later, they calculated the best time for us to hook up, my period and all, and we did.

Payton: And the same thing the second time?

Morales: Same thing. And I lost the baby again. Only this one was farther along–second trimester. I could feel him kicking around.

Payton: You're sure it was a boy?

Morales: No, but–I had that feeling, you know. I don't like thinking about it, because even though part of the deal was that I had to give up the baby, I was feeling something already. Maternal instinct, I guess they call it. I had a name picked out in my head, too. Antonio. Tony. Like my grandfather. Even though they wouldn't let me see him again, I still . . .

Payton: You all right?

Morales: Sorry.

Payton: That's okay. You want to take a break?

Morales: No. Bastards. You're gonna nail 'em, right?

Payton: To the wall.

Morales: Good. See when I lost the baby–the babies–I was the only one upset by it. I mean, none of them seemed to care. Almost like the first two didn't matter.

Payton: The third time was different, though.

Morales: Way different. From the beginning.

Payton: Go on.

Morales: It wasn't John who got me pregnant that time.

Payton: Who was it?

Morales: I don't know.

Payton: You don't know?

Morales: I think they drugged me. I remember going in to see them, and them running some tests, and then—wow. They must have slipped me something, 'cause I was lying in the hospital bed there, and the next thing I knew, I was flying. I mean, all high and shit, you know. Maybe I was hallucinating, 'cause I thought I was someplace else entirely.

Payton: Where?

Morales: A big room somewhere—a chamber, or something. And there was a party going on around me, a costume party, people in robes and weird makeup. John was there, and some other people I recognized from the institute, and—

Payton: Sandeman?

Morales: No, I don't remember seeing him, but—I have to say that I don't remember a hell of a lot clearly. I do remember the end, though.

Payton: Go on.

Morales: I don't like to think about it. John was just looking on, with this big smile on his face, and these other people were holding me down, and then this man—he had a hood over his face, so I don't know for sure, but I think it might have been the old man from Sandeman's office. He . . .

Payton: He assaulted you.

Morales: Yeah. That's the polite way of putting it.

Payton: I'm sorry.

Morales: That wasn't the worst, though. The worst thing was after that—they didn't let me go. Kept me in that place, in their hospital, for nine months. It was like a freaking insane asylum, you know? I saw all these other girls there, young girls just like me, they were all pregnant, too. And they kept me so doped up half the time, I didn't know what was what.

Payton: You think you could identify any of the other girls you saw there?

Morales: Maybe. I could try.

Payton: Good. I'm getting some pictures from a friend of mine tomorrow—we'll go through them.

Morales: All right.

Payton: So how did you finally escape?

Morales: Somebody screwed up and left my door open. This was after I had the baby. After they took him from me. God. I wish I'd never . . .

Payton: What were they going to do with the child?

Morales: I don't know. They never said. Funny.

Payton: What?

Morales: I just remembered something. Sandeman. He was the last one I saw that night—that night I escaped. I remember him coming in and standing over my bed. Smiling at me.

Payton: Like you did good?

Morales: No. More like the kind of smile somebody gives you when they want to make you feel better. Like he was on my side. Hey—maybe he's the one who left the door open for me.

Payton: That doesn't make sense, though, does it? He was one of the people in charge.

Morales: Yeah. I guess you're right. So you going to put all this in the paper?

Payton: That's right. They're never going to do this to anyone—ever again.

Morales: Good. Because . . .

Payton: It's all right, Miss Morales. Why don't we stop now.

TO: payton@postexpress.com

FROM: editorial@postexpress.com

DATE: 8/13/96

RE: DAVENPORT/LEGAL REVIEW

Cowards!

It's a hell of a piece, Brian, but we're holding off on publication pending outside legal review. The suits here are worried--Davenport has deep, deep pockets, and a propensity to sue.

You're sure about your facts, right? Any way to confirm the girl's story?

TO: editorial@postexpress.com

FROM: payton@postexpress.com

DATE: 8/13/96

RE: DAVENPORT/LEGAL REVIEW

Christ, Mike, you've got to be kidding me!!!!

We've got the physical evidence from the cops, confirmation from the institute she was a patient there--what do you want, videotape? This is bullshit.

TO: payton@postexpress.com

FROM: editorial@postexpress.com

DATE: 8/13/96

RE: DAVENPORT/LEGAL REVIEW

Hey, it's not what I want, Brian. It's what Mr. Dozier wants--he signs the paychecks. And he wants outside counsel to review the piece. That'll happen overnight, and I think they'll see it just like you do--just like I do.

Relax. You did good work.

FROM THE LAW OFFICES OF

WEINREICH, KOHLER, AND MCKINLEY

250 PARK AVENUE SUITE 24G NEW YORK NEW YORK 10034

August 14, 1996

Montgomery Dozier
Publisher
Post Express
2 Park Avenue
New York NY 10016

Dear Mr. Dozier:

As you requested, I've completed my review of the article by Mr. Payton regarding Davenport Genetics Institute. While there are portions of the piece that are certainly verifiable, it is my expert opinion that at this time you should not proceed with publication. At such a time as you can obtain third-party confirmation of Ms. Morales's story, I suggest resubmitting the piece for review.

I understand that due to the exclusive nature of your reporter's relationship with Ms. Morales, public interest in this piece will be tremendous. Let me suggest—though by no means do I pretend to be expert in your business—that a shorter article detailing the progress of the investigation itself would be more appropriate at this time.

I'm sorry to be the bearer of bad news here. No doubt your reporter put a lot of work into this—but as always, my feeling in these types of situations is to err on the side of caution.

My best to your family, and please don't hesitate to call me if you have any questions on this matter.

All best,

George McKinley
Senior Partner

GM/db

TO: FILE
FROM: PAYTON
DATE: 8/15/96
RE: MORALES INTERVIEW, SESSION 5

Payton: All right, the recorder's going, just calm down and let's–

Morales: Calm down? You want me to calm down? They're watching me all the time, Brian! All the time–I go out, and there's two of them in a car across the street. I go for the paper, and there's one standing at the bus stop. They're at the grocery store, and they're at the gas station, and–

Payton: Calm down, Josie. You're starting to sound paranoid.

Morales: Paranoid? You're goddamn right I'm paranoid! Look what they did–they stopped you from publishing your article, they got you fired from the paper–

Payton: They didn't get me fired, Josie. My boss just told me to take a leave of absence until I calmed down.

Morales: It comes out to the same thing. You're screwed, and I'm screwed. Heh.

Payton: No. Listen, they're not the only paper in town. I know people at the *Voice* and they might–

Morales: Don't. Just don't.

Payton: What do you mean?

Morales: I mean, it'll just be more of the same. I can't stop them, you can't stop them–no one can.

Payton: Don't be silly. Of course we can stop them–this is the United States of America.

Morales: Doesn't matter.

Payton: Josie? What is it?

Morales: Give me a minute, all right? Just give me a minute, I'll be fine.

Morales: The old man called me last night.

Payton: What?

Morales: The one from the institute. I know it was him. He told me the baby was doing fine. Not to worry about him. But–he said he was worried about me. Running out on their "expert" care–what might happen to me.

Payton: That bastard. I'm calling the cops.

Morales: No, Brian. Don't.

Payton: What do you mean? This is the proof–he threatened you.

Morales: Doesn't matter. I'm leaving town.

Payton: What?

Morales: I have a brother in St. Louis–I'm going to see him. Stay with him. Move there.

Payton: Oh, Josie, don't. Don't let them chase you off. Don't let them win.

Morales: I don't care about that anymore. I don't care about the baby, or anything. I just–I'm scared, Brian. I don't want to die.

Payton: You're not going to–Josie, come back here, will you? Josie!

[Door slams.]

NEW YORK POST EXPRESS

WEDNESDAY, AUGUST 21, 1996

Institute's Accuser a Suicide

by Steve Nathanson
Exclusive to the *Post Express*

ange

Brooklyn—Josephine Morales, the young woman who made headlines last week by accusing a prestigious Long Island research facility of kidnapping her, committed suicide yesterday evening by jumping to her death from the roof of a Cobble Hill brownstone.

New York City Police, called to the scene at 7:30 p.m., discovered Morales's body on the sidewalk outside 325 Wyckoff Street, and pronounced her dead on the scene. The determination of suicide was made after interviewing an eyewitness and the examination of forensic evidence.

Morales, who had been staying with a friend in the building, made headlines last week by accusing the prestigious Davenport Genetics Institute of kidnapping her and forcing her to have a baby against her will. Subsequent investigation revealed her charges to be groundless; one detective, speaking on condition of anonymity, stated that Morales's statements to them were confusing and contradictory, and indicated to him some sort of substance abuse.

Contacted early this morning, the Davenport Institute released the following statement on Morales's death. "Loss of life is tragic, and doubly so when it happens to one so young and under such terrible circumstances. Josephine was a troubled soul whom we were trying to help; sadly, our efforts were for naught. Whatever part we may have played in bringing about the mental state that caused her death we apologize greatly for, and our hearts go out to her friends and family."

Morales was twenty years old, and a resident of Elizabeth, New Jersey. She is survived by her parents, Benjamin and Olivia, also of Elizabeth, and older brother Steven, of St. Louis, Missouri.

Funeral arr- -ments are pending.

TO: payton@postexpress.com

FROM: editorial@postexpress.com

DATE: 8/23/96

RE: MORALES

What, have you lost your mind? No way, Brian. I know you got close to the girl, and I'm sorry about what happened, but that doesn't give us license to publish the piece, or anything remotely hinting at Davenport's involvement in her suicide. Got that? Suicide, not murder.

Drop it. Take another week, and go someplace warm and sunny. Clear your head, and come back ready to work.

TO: editorial@postexpress.com

FROM: payton@postexpress.com

DATE: 8/23/96

RE: WORK

I'm ready to work now, Mike. You ready to see what I've been working on? I found another girl--she confirms everything Morales was saying. The fifty thousand dollars to have a kid, the miscarriages--she bailed after the second one, without telling the institute what she was planning to do. Probably the only reason she's alive today.

Let's do this, Mike. Let's nail those bastards.

TO: payton@postexpress.com

FROM: editorial@postexpress.com

DATE: 8/23/96

RE: WORK

So who's your other source, Brian? It's got to be somebody more reputable than Morales--did you see the hospital records the police just released on her? She was psycho.

TO: editorial@postexpress.com

FROM: payton@postexpress.com

DATE: 8/23/96

RE: WORK

Convenient timing on the release of those records, huh? They're bullshit, is why. A smear campaign against a dead girl. A murdered girl.

And sorry, but I have to hold on to the name of this source.

TO: editorial@postexpress.com

FROM: payton@postexpress.com

DATE: 8/24/96

RE: WORK

That's a chickenshit way to do things, Mike. I thought we were friends. Friends don't fire you by leaving a phone message.

I'm beginning to think they got to you too, friend. Is that it? Is that what happened?

Show me you got some balls left, Mike. Call me at home tonight.

TO: lcale@pfpfree.net

FROM: bpayton58@rcn.net

DATE: 5/6/21

RE: <No subject was specified>

No, he never did call, Mr. Cale. You think you know people, but under pressure . . . some of them just fold up like an accordion. Anyway . . .

Davenport went on, business as usual, until right after the Pulse. Then they relocated—I was never able to find out where. But this Sandeman guy you're asking about, he left way before that. And not on good terms, either. I know because I was still trying to work the story. There was this lab tech I got friendly with, and one time I asked her about Sandeman. Mistake. She hushed up tighter than a drum and said I shouldn't mention his name again—not around her, not around anyone connected to the institute. If I knew what was good for me.

Makes me wonder if there wasn't some truth to Josie's thought, that he was the one who helped her escape.

As far as the other girl goes, my other source—I'm sorry. Like I told Mike, I made her a promise.

TO: bpayton58@rcn.net

FROM: lcale@pfpfree.net

DATE: 5/6/21

RE: The Conclave

Mr. Payton, I appreciate your honesty, and feel you deserve some in return. After you hear what I have to say—as crazy as it may sound to you—I'm hoping you'll give me that girl's name.

What happened to Josie Morales—and to the other girls she mentioned—has been going on for a long, long time. Thousands of years, perhaps.

I'm attaching some pictures to this e-mail. They're from a Kiloma Indian burial site, dating back to the early 1800s. There's a story that goes with these pictures—a story about a young Kiloma girl kidnapped from the tribe by a group

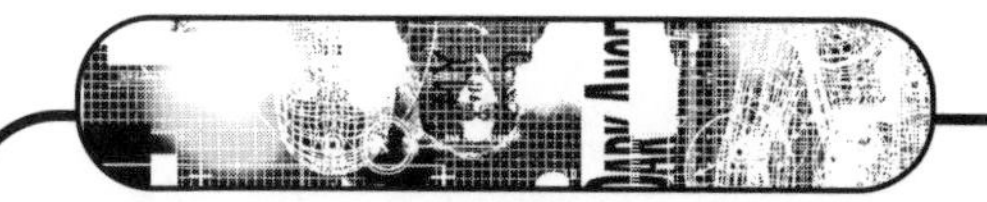

of fur traders. Kidnapped, and forced to have a child by a boy the traders had brought with them. A boy described as not much more than fourteen years old—and already well over six feet tall.

The Kiloma girl gave birth to a child, all right—a terribly deformed baby. That's the first skeleton you see. The girl was forced to try again. This time, the infant was healthy—but the traders killed it anyway. The crushed skull, in the second picture. And the third time . . . the traders were satisfied. They took the child away—and killed the mother.

But I don't think these people were traders at all, Mr. Payton. I think they were part of the same group that a century later was running Davenport. The same group that killed Josie. And they're out there right now, doing it all again.

Help me stop them.

Give me the girl's name.

DECRYPTION: SECURE 8 DECRYPTION STAMP: 5/8/21 ORIGINAL TRANSCRIPT: 5/06/21 L = Cale, Logan, M = Chantal, Marisa

M: Hello?

L: Hello. I'm looking for Marisa Chantal.

M: This is Marisa. Who is this?

L: Ms. Chantal, my name is Logan Cale. I was given your name by Brian Payton. Do you remember Mr. Payton?

L: Ms. Chantal?

M: I don't think I want to talk to you Mr. Cale. Good-bye.

L: Don't hang up. Please. People's lives are at stake here. A lot of people's lives.

M: Including mine. Like I said, I—

L: Listen to me. I'm not going to ask you to say anything on the record. I'm not going to ask you to testify anywhere, about anything. I just want information, Ms. Chantal. That's all.

M: How do I know who you are? How do I know you're not with them?

L: I have your phone number, Ms. Chantal. I can easily find out where you live. Why would I bother calling you if I wanted to hurt you?

M: Maybe you're right.

L: So will you talk to me?

M: All right. Hold on a minute.

M: We can talk now. I had to change phones.

L: Thank you. I won't waste your time with a lot of questions. So I'm assuming you remember Mr. Payton. Then can you confirm the story Josephine Morales told?

M: Yes. That poor girl.

L: There were a lot of other girls involved as well, weren't there?

M: I don't know about a lot of others. I saw only her, when I went in for some tests. My God—I can't believe how stupid I was. To take money to bear a child.

L: What made you decide not to go through with it?

M: The second time I miscarried, I met one of their doctors—a man I hadn't seen before. He scared me to death.

L: How so?

M: I can't explain it, really. Just his presence. I suddenly knew that whatever they intended for me, it wasn't good. That I would never see the money they promised.

L: Who was this doctor? Do you remember his name?

M: Schuler. Dr. Mark Schuler.

L: Can you describe Dr. Schuler?

M: Tall, thin—he was old. My God, he was very, very old.

FILE CONTINUES

Beyond whatever legitimate laboratory work they were doing, it was clear now that the Davenport Institute had been a cover for White's breeding cult. What they'd done to Morales and the other girls—what they'd tried to do to Marissa Chantal—that was the same pattern that had been repeated over centuries. Repeated right here in Seattle, too, with Ames White and his own wife, Wendy. And their son Ray, whom I'd helped escape all that.

I still wasn't any closer to finding Sandeman, though—or to figuring out what the symbols on Max's body meant. What the "shroud of death" referred to.

Except now I realized that maybe a change in approach might be called for.

The old man who scared Marisa Chantal—Dr. Schuler—he was very likely the old man who'd assaulted Morales. Very possibly the Marcus from Sandeman's letter, as well.

Almost certainly, he would know what the symbols meant.

Maybe, I decided, I should try finding him.

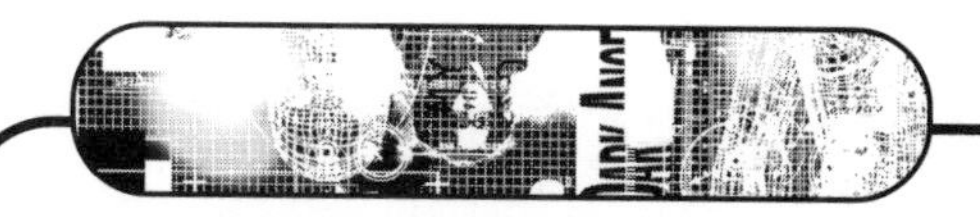

TO: iionly@pfpfree.net

FROM: seb2009@pfpfree.net

DATE: 5/7/21

RE: Schuler

That name rings a bell, though for the life of me I can't remember why. At any rate . . .

Trying all variants—Mark, Marcus, Markus, M. Schuler, M. Schyuler—I come up empty. I will keep looking, though—and thinking.

TO: iionly@pfpfree.net

FROM: gatekeeper@pfpfree.net

DATE: 5/7/21

RE: Schuler

<no subject was specified>

Nada.

TO: iionly@pfpfree.net

FROM: dazzler@pfpfree.net

DATE: 5/6/21

RE: Davenport Genetics Institute

This is weird. I made a mistake and entered search parameters 1900-present instead of 2000-present.

Look what came back.

It can't be the same guy—can it?

INVESTIGATION OF NAZI PARTY ACTIVITIES AND INVESTIGATION OF CERTAIN OTHER UN-AMERICAN ACTIVITIES

PUBLIC HEARINGS

BEFORE THE

SPECIAL COMMITTEE ON UN-AMERICAN ACTIVITIES

HOUSE OF REPRESENTATIVES

SEVENTY-THIRD CONGRESS

SECOND SESSION

AT NEW YORK CITY, N.Y.
October 30 and 31, 1934

HEARINGS No. 79-N.Y.-15

United States
Government Publications Committee
Washington: 1934

INVESTIGATION OF UN-AMERICAN ACTIVITIES

WEDNESDAY OCTOBER 31 1934

House of Representatives
Subcommittee of the Special
Committee on Un-American Activities

New York City

The subcommittee met at 10:30 A.M. in the Vanderbilt Auditorium, Forty-third Street, New York , the Hon. Charles H. McIntyre (chairman) presiding. Present also were the Hon. George Honeycutt; the committee counsel, the Hon. Lewis Chimes; and the official interpreter, Mr. Philip Boehm.

THE CHAIRMAN. The committee will be in order. We will call Dr. Schuler.

TESTIMONY OF DOCTOR MARKUS SCHULER

(The witness was duly sworn by the chairman.)

THE CHAIRMAN. Your full name is Markus Schuler?

DR. SCHULER. Yes.

THE CHAIRMAN. And are you a citizen of this country?

DR. SCHULER. Yes. I received my papers ten years ago. I have lived in America for the last forty years.

THE CHAIRMAN. You were not born here, though?

DR. SCHULER. No sir. I was born in Germany.

THE CHAIRMAN. And how old are you now, sir?

DR. SCHULER. I am sixty-eight years old.

THE CHAIRMAN. If you will permit me, Doctor—you seem in remarkable condition for a man of your age.

DR. SCHULER. Thank you, Mr. Chairman. I am very fortunate to have the benefit of good genetics.

THE CHAIRMAN. In fact, it is genetics with which we are concerned today, sir. Specifically, your activities as a member of the World Eugenics League.

MR. CHIMES. Mr. Chairman?

THE CHAIRMAN. Yes, Mr. Chimes.

MR. CHIMES. I wish to note for the record exhibit 32A, which has been submitted to this committee. A document describing the goals and activities of the World Eugenics League.

THE CHAIRMAN. So noted. Dr. Schuler, I direct your attention to the document Mr. Chimes mentioned. You are a member of the organization referred to therein, sir?

DR. SCHULER. Yes, sir. I am one of its directors.

THE CHAIRMAN. Can you summarize its activities for this committee?

DR. SCHULER. I will be happy to. In brief, the World Eugenics League is devoted to the improvement of the human condition through the scientific application of genetic principles.

MR. HONEYCUTT. Excuse me—Mr. Chairman?

THE CHAIRMAN. The floor is yours, Mr. Honeycutt.

MR. HONEYCUTT. Thank you sir. Now Dr. Schuler, could you elaborate on that explanation a little—for those of us here, like myself, who are not as well versed in the sciences?

DR. SCHULER. Of course. Mr. Honeycutt, are you familiar with names Darwin and Mendel?

MR. HONEYCUTT. Darwin I've heard of, all right. But that other fellow . . .

DR. SCHULER. Mendel. He is the father of genetics, sir. It was he who proved that physical traits such as height, weight, hair color, among many others, are inherited characteristics. We in the league have discovered traits beyond the physical that are inherited, as well.

MR. HONEYCUTT. Such as . . .

DR. SCHULER. Intelligence. Physical attractiveness. Longevity. All these traits can be bred into the race.

MR. HONEYCUTT. I don't know. Sounds to me like you're talking about cows, or racehorses, more than human beings.

DR. SCHULER. The principles are the same.

MR. HONEYCUTT: But you're not doing any actual experiments on human beings?

DR. SCHULER. Experiments is the wrong word, sir. We encourage selective breeding, but we do not favor any sort of coerced behavior.

MR. HONEYCUTT. That's good to know.

THE CHAIRMAN. Now, Dr. Schuler—you are aware that the German Nazi Party and Chancellor Hitler are also in favor of this—this kind of breeding program you're talking about?

DR. SCHULER. Yes, sir. Though I must point out that their program is totally without scientific merit. It is based on a myth of German racial superiority. No scientific data exist to support such superiority. Over the last year, the World Eugenics League has—

as you gentlemen are aware—funded advertising that notes the difference between true eugenics and the absurd propaganda Mr. Hitler's party spouts.

MR. CHIMES. Identified here as exhibit 32B, Mr. Chairman.

THE CHAIRMAN. Thank you, Mr. Chimes. Now Dr. Schuler—to return to the question of the Nazi Party. I must ask you, sir—are you now, or have you ever been a member of the Nazi Party?

DR. SCHULER. No, sir. I consider that group and its leaders contemptuous. I find their racial purity laws violently disagreeable.

THE CHAIRMAN. This committee appreciates your honesty, Doctor.

MR. HONEYCUTT. I'd like to ask a few more questions of Dr. Schuler, regarding some of the folks that work with you in this World Eugenics League.

DR. SCHULER. I am happy to cooperate with the committee in whatever way I can.

MR. HONEYCUTT. I appreciate that, sir. Let me start by referring you to the membership list you've provided to this committee.

MR. CHIMES. That's 32C, Mr. Chairman.

THE CHAIRMAN. Thank you, Mr. Chimes.

MR. HONEYCUTT. Yes, thank you Mr. Chimes. Now Dr. Schuler, looks to me like a lot of German names here. I wonder if you wouldn't mind sharing with us some of what you know about these people.

TO: dazzler@pfpfree.net

FROM: iionly@pfpfree.net

DATE: 5/6/21

RE: Schuler

According to the testimony, he was sixty-eight in 1934. That would make him 155 years old now. Unlikely. But impossible?

Over the last couple of years, I've seen some things that have caused me to redefine that word. So I'm not ruling anything out.

TO: iionly@pfpfree.net

FROM: seb2009@pfpfree.net

DATE: 5/7/21

RE: Schuler

mckinley press conf.4/2/2021 -- source: f:/tempfiles/net/csatcps/4282021/mckin.jpg

Now I remember why his name sounded so familiar.

I've met him.

It was last March, at a fund-raising dinner for Senator McKinley downtown—ten thousand dollars a plate. I was there as a speaker on the program, to talk about the senator's plan to bring high-tech industry back to Seattle. It sounds good on paper, but of course the final program will bear no resemblance to what actually comes out of Congress. Still, they paid me good money to show up and talk about it.

Let me tell you, everyone who was anyone was there—Mayor Steckler and his wife, Governor Chalfont from Oregon, Johnny and Gina Liberti, and of course McKinley. He was on the dais at the front of the room.

When I went up to speak, my escort introduced me to the senator. We exchanged small talk, then McKinley introduced me to the man on his left. An elderly gentleman named Schuler. No last name, no first name, no title, no information about who or what he was. We said hello, and that was all.

After I spoke, I returned to my seat. Several times during the evening, I saw Schuler and McKinley talk. The nature of their relationship was clear to me.

Schuler spoke. McKinley listened.

Teacher and pupil. Master and servant.

You've seen McKinley on TV. He's been chairing the hearings on the "transgenic threat."

He used Ames White's testimony before his committee to transform the search for the transgenics into a witch-hunt.

He may very well be the same McKinley who stopped Payton from publishing his exposé on the breeding cult and Davenport, over twenty years ago.

He may, in fact, be a member of the cult himself.

But I have no way to find out.

I'm cut off from everything now—deaf, dumb, and blind to my operatives, the Informant Net, and the world outside.

So now it's up to you. You have the information you need. You have my sources. Good luck.

Peace. Out.

—EYES ONLY

ACKNOWLEDGMENTS

First of all, special thanks to:

Steve Saffel, my editor—for introducing me to the world of *Dark Angel,* encouraging me to run fast and free within it, and keeping me focused on the finish line when my attention wandered.

Wendy Chesebrough at Lightstorm—for providing the inside scoop on post-Pulse America, twenty-four/seven, weekends and home telephone number included.

Debbie Olshan at Fox—for the cheerfully supplied, constantly arriving stream of Airborne Express packages—videotapes, photos, graphics, etc., etc., etc.

And of course . . . James Cameron, Charles Eglee, and the staff of *Dark Angel,* for inspirations visual, intellectual, and emotional.

Thanks also . . .

At Ballantine Books: Denise Fitzer, Barbara Greenberg, Colleen Lindsay, Betsy Mitchell, Colette Russen, and of course, Gina Centrello (queen of the ten-dollar hamburger).

At Laura Lindgren Design, Inc.: Laura Lindgren, for reasons obvious to anyone holding this book in their hands.

Also: Max Allan Collins, Dana Hayward, and the numerous friends and acquaintances who helped me "flesh out" the *Dark Angel* Universe.

Finally, thanks to the on-line *Dark Angel* community, for another kind of inspiration. This book is really for you all—I hope you like it.

ABOUT THE AUTHOR

D. A. Stern is the author of several previous works of fiction and nonfiction, including *Black Dawn, Your Secrets Are My Business* (with Kevin McKeown), and *Enterprise: What Price Honor.* He lives in western Massachusetts with his family and two very pointy dogs. For more info:

http://more.at/dastern